NEW YORK TIMES BESTSELLING AUTHOR

JA HUSS

ABOUT THE BOOK

It's Christmas Eve and everyone's in Vail to celebrate. The secrets were revealed, the problems all solved, and the danger has been over for years now. So why are Ronin, Ford, and Spencer so worried about the future? Family life comes with its own set of problems. None of which can be solved with guns, or fight moves, or clues. In fact, it's their super smart kids who swoop in to save the day this time.

A fun, flirty, final HEA epilogue to one of the most loved set of characters ever.

🏠 Found Family · 🔒 Forced Proximity
🌲 Holiday Romance · 🛡️ Overprotective Dads
💘 First Love · 💕 Friends to Lovers
💘 He Falls First · 📖 Multiple POV
🍀 Grumpy Sunshine · 🕯️ Happily Ever After

HAPPILY EVER AFTER
ROOK & RONIN #9
Copyright © 2015 by JA Huss
ISBN: 978-1944475000

This is a work of fiction. Names, characters, businesses, places, events
and incidents are either the products of the author's imagination or used
in a fictitious manner. Any resemblance to actual persons, living or dead,
or actual events is purely coincidental.

Edited by RJ Locksley
Cover Design by JA Huss

FIVE

"Five?"

Kate is calling me from the bottom of the stairs. I'm stuck up in the attic bedroom in the Vail vacation mansion with Oliver, as usual. He's still snoring. Kids. They love Christmas. He was so excited last night, he stayed up talking me to death until three AM.

"Five?" Kate yells again.

I look in the bathroom mirror and smooth an out-of-place hair, then straighten my tie.

"Why didn't you answer me?" Kate asks, coming up behind me. She's clearly annoyed with my indifference, because she has one hand on her hip. "I've been calling you." She stops short and covers her mouth as she laughs. "You are *not* wearing that."

"I'm busy, Kate. I have adult things on my mind."

When I look over at her she's just giving me that dumbfounded stare. "I'm older than you."

"Age is not what makes a person mature."

"Anyway," she says, sighing and blowing some of her dark bangs out of her eyes. "Rook is making us all breakfast. Pancakes!" This lights up her face. Kids love their pancakes too. "But seriously, Five. No one wears suits to Christmas Eve breakfast. It's stupid."

"It says upwardly mobile."

"That's stupid too. No one wants to look like they're going on a job interview at family breakfast." She pauses, looking me up and down with a critical eye. "You know she'd like you more if you weren't so weird."

"I have no idea to whom you are referring. And I'm not weird."

Kate snickers. "OK. But she's my best friend, you know. Rory tells me everything and she thinks you're weird."

"She does not," I say, spinning around so I can look Kate in the eyes. "Princess Shrike is my one true love. She knows this. I know this. And one day, when we are of legal age to marry, the world will know this."

Kate sighs. "I was kidding. Well, a little bit. She has remarked about the suits though, Five. For real. Don't wear it. I'm not steering you wrong here. I'm trying to help."

"I agree," five-year-old Oliver says from behind Kate, still rubbing the sleep out of his eyes. "Lose the suit and put on the snowmen, Rutherford the Fifth. Trust me, I live with her. She likes this stuff. She's always telling me how cute I am in these." He points to his flannel character pajama pants.

"First of all," I say, putting up a finger, "do not call me

Rutherford the Fifth. Second, I don't *have* snowman pants. Third, suits always say normal."

"Wait here," Kate says with a sigh.

"Whatever," I say, turning back to the mirror to check my tie again.

"You should take our advice, Five," Oliver says. "I'm a girl expert. I have five sisters. I live with them. Rory likes boys who wear t-shirts. Like that Marshall kid in her class."

"Marshall?" I squint at myself in the mirror, my mind whirring to try and place a kid named Marshall. "Who is Marshall?"

"Quarterback for the varsity team," Oliver says. "She went to the library with him last week."

"Hmmm." I hate not being in the same school as her anymore. She's at a charter school in Fort Collins and I'm commuting to University of Denver twice a week. Why do I have to be so smart?

"Yeah, Marshall something. Do you want me to find out his last name so you can hack into his email like you did the last boy she was talking to?"

"Jesus, Oliver. You have some imagination. I don't hack things." I do hack things, but I'm not allowed to hack things, so Spencer's big-mouth son needs to keep his mouth shut. "But I'll take that last name if you can get it."

Oliver gives me a conspiratorial wink just as Kate comes bounding up the attic steps again.

"Here," she says, thrusting a present at me. "You'll have one less thing under the tree, but it's more of a Christmas Eve gift anyway."

I take the gift bag filled with bright red tissue paper and peer inside. Pajama pants. "No," I say, handing it back to Kate.

"Seriously, Five. You'll look cute." And then she reaches up and messes up my hair. "Girls like that too. And you should stop shaving those three stubbly things growing on your chin. Girls like a shadow."

"You have no idea what you're talking about, Kate. I know what Princess likes. Me. I don't have to wear weird pants or look like a vagrant. I just need to be me."

"I saw her staring at Marshall when he was at football camp last summer," Oliver says. "Princess was at the cheerleading camp across the field and—"

"What?" I was at Stanford all last summer. "She went to cheer camp? Cheer camp with football-playing boys?" I almost can't take it. "I thought she was riding all summer?"

"See," Kate says. "You don't even know her anymore. I'm sure you were best friends back at Saint Joseph's, Five, but she's grown up a lot since seventh grade."

"She's only in ninth grade now, Kate. It's not like I missed much."

"Marshall is in eleventh grade," Oliver says through a sleepy yawn.

"What? What the hell is wrong with Spencer? How can he allow his daughter to associate with an older man?"

Kate shakes the bag of flannel pants at me. "Put them on. She does like that guy, Five. He asked her to Winter Formal, but we were going out of town that weekend to talk to those horse catalog people, so she had to say no."

I just stare at the bag. "Flannel?"

"And a t-shirt," Oliver says. "Shrike Bikes, if you've got one."

"I'm telling you," Kate says. "She likes you, Five. She's always liked you. But you're moving on without her. It's not her who's leaving you behind next semester. Oxford is a long way away. You won't even recognize her when you come back in the summer. *If* you come back."

"If?"

"Please, Five. You're smart. You know that you'll love it there. You know you'll get involved in all sorts of nerdy academic things and coming home might not be a priority after you get settled. You're going to be living the life of an adult. Rory is a freshman in high school. She's not interested in growing up so fast. Not like that, anyway."

I don't ask what *that* means. I know what it means. She's going to do all her teen things without me. I'm going to be thousands of miles away all engrossed in computer engineering, and she's going to be thinking about football games and Marshall. It's research labs and college life for me and dances and note passing for her.

I take the bag of pajama pants from Kate and close the bathroom door to change.

When I get downstairs Princess is laughing and joking with Sparrow and Kate as they eat their pancakes sitting at the kitchen island. Rook is flitting around filling plates and the little kids are sitting at the kitchenette table near the window where there is a clear view of the ski slopes.

I feel self-conscious in this new outfit. I want to hide

behind my suit and tie. I want to hide behind the facade of normal so the only girl I've ever wanted won't see too deep inside me.

But when she turns and takes me in I know that Kate was right. My new look delights her. I can see it in her bright blue eyes.

"Five." She laughs. But it's not a laugh that says 'you look ridiculous.' It's a laugh that says, "You look..." I wait for it. "Cool. I dig the penguins." She looks me over, taking a full two or three seconds to do it. "And the bedhead." She giggles. "It suits you."

I glance over at Kate, sitting just to Princess' right, and she gives me an I-told-you-so smile.

"Thanks," I say, letting out a breath of relief. If Kate is right and Rory is thinking of liking a guy who is not me, then I need to step up my game. I need to get her full attention every time I walk into a room. My eyes get stuck on her perfect lips and I wonder briefly if she's ever kissed that boy she likes.

No. I'm pretty sure Spencer would walk over to that kid's house and threaten him with a shotgun if she has. She hasn't kissed him. Yet.

And with that my mission becomes clear.

I need to kiss Princess Rory and I need to do that today.

2

RONIN

"Hey," Rook whispers in my ear. "Wake up."

"Hmmmmm," I growl. "What time is it?" I crack one eye open. "It's still dark. We just went to bed."

"No." Rook laughs. "It's seven."

"Practically night time."

"I made you breakfast, so sit up," Rook says, sitting down on the bed next to me.

"Since when?" I laugh. Rook is perfect in all ways, but she and I have never been on the same time clock. She is not a morning person.

"It's Christmas Eve. You know I love Christmas Eve. So I just wanted to cook for the kids. And I made pancakes. Your favorite."

"Yeah, you love to *sleep* on Christmas Eve. Ronnie always makes breakfast when we're in Vail. She's a kitchen control freak here at the mountain house."

Rook tsks her tongue. "She was up with Cindy. She's

teething. So Ash helped her last night so she could get some sleep and I said I'd make breakfast."

"Oh, that sucks." I reach around and grab Rook by her waist and pull her down next to me. "Thank you," I say, kissing her on the cheek and sliding my hand up to her breast. She's wearing one of my old t-shirts and some shorts. She knows I love the shorts. "Let's take advantage of the chowing kids and get our kinky on."

She grins at me and then reaches over to the side table where the tray of food is. "Strawberries? Antoine had a fruit basket delivered this morning. The doorbell woke up the pack of princesses. That's why I'm awake. I'm surprised you didn't hear Ford's face-eaters."

"Mmmm. Forget the kids, feed me, Rook."

I catch a mischievous grin as she leans over to grab a strawberry, my hand never leaving her soft breast. I twist her nipple a little and that makes her close her eyes and draw in a breath.

"Open," she says, bringing the berry to my mouth.

I take a bite and chew. The sun is just starting to rise and the pink dawn casts a hazy light over her face. We have been together for sixteen Christmases. Sixteen. Sparrow is almost fourteen and Starling is six. They are just like her. So pretty. So sweet. So perfect. And they have spent every Christmas in this house that I bought with Spencer and Ford once things settled down back. I love coming to Vail for the holidays. And we spend weeks at a time out here in the summer when the girls are out of school.

The house is massive, but it has to be to hold our

families. Spencer has six kids with the addition of Cindy last spring. Add in our two and Ford's two and that's ten kids and six adults who call this place home. It's big enough though. Eight bedrooms, eleven bathrooms and eight thousand square feet of living space if you add in the basement.

Luckily there are two wings and most of the kids sleep on the other side of the house so we can have some privacy. Spencer and Ronnie have the master and since they always seem to have a new baby, they remodeled the giant walk-in closet into a nursery for easy access. But all the bedrooms are big and have their own en suite bathrooms.

And Rook and I lucked out with a large terrace off our bedroom. It has a hot tub that we enjoy every Christmas Eve. God, I can't wait for that moment tonight when we climb into the hot tub.

We have a typical Vail mountain home with long wooden beams running across the ceiling, a floor-to-ceiling stone fireplace in the living room, and a chef's kitchen for Ronnie, since she's the cook around here.

"It's quiet down there," I say. "I think we could have a quickie in the shower."

"I'll run the water," Rook says, jumping up to do that.

"Hmmmm." I hate to be suspicious, but none of this is adding up. Usually Rook sleeps like the dead. She never gets up early and I can't recall a single time when she's brought me breakfast in bed. "Hey, Rook?" I call out over the sound of the running water.

"Yeah?" she calls back, and then steps out of the bathroom naked.

"Jesus. You're in the mood or what?" I grin and chuckle.

"*So* in the mood, Ronin. Get up, let's start this day right."

"But…" I look over at the plate of pancakes. They are all misshapen and broken. That makes me love her even more. She can't make a round pancake if her life depended on it. "The food will get cold."

"I'll make more," she says, so easy-going.

"Hmmmm."

"Hmm what?" She cocks her head at me and leans against the bathroom wall, like she's flirting with me. "Come on. Don't keep me waiting." And then she turns back to the shower and disappears.

I throw the covers off and stuff a pancake in my mouth before following her in, my shirt already over my head and my fingers on the waistband of my shorts, tugging them down as I walk.

I've got morning wood, so I'm all over this invitation.

She's already under the water, sopping wet from head to toe. Her long dark hair hangs down her back and she looks just like the girl I met back in Antoine's studio in Five Points.

"Come on," Rook says, encouraging me as she fondles her breasts. "Before the minions want our attention."

"Well, you've definitely got *my* attention." She's never been a prude, but the last time she tried to seduce me was… shit, years ago, I think. I step into the shower and she starts washing me with soap. "Mrs. Flynn, what is going on?"

"What?" she asks innocently. She's got those big doe eyes going on, and her shoulders are shrugging. "I just want some alone time before the hustle and bustle of the holidays overtakes us."

Her hands drag the soap up and down my body, from my chest to my abs, and I have no choice. I'm under her spell. All I can do is stand there and enjoy it. A few seconds into this and she drops the soap and wraps her hand around my cock, squeezing it until I get even harder.

I moan a little as she pumps me slowly, and then her other hand pushes against my chest until I back up and have to take a seat on the bench. She drops into a squat, my eyes seeking out her pussy as she opens her legs for me.

"Jesus, Rook. What's got into you?"

"You're complaining?" she asks, before taking the head of my cock in her mouth.

"Oh, fuck," I moan, leaning back against the cold tile wall. "Well," I say, my breathing heavy, "whatever it is, I like it."

"Hmmm," she says, moaning as she continues to suck me.

I grab her wet hair and pull her towards me, then scoot down a little on the bench seat so I can fully enjoy this morning treat. She takes me deep and I hiss in a breath, fisting her hair. "Yeah," I say. "I like that."

She withdraws and then stand and positions herself over my cock, her ass brushing against my thighs. "Good," she whispers over the running water. "Good," she repeats as she lowers herself down onto me.

I open my eyes just in time to see her close hers, and then she sits down all the way, my cock filling her up.

"I love you so much," she says.

"I love you too," I say, my heart racing as her breathing picks up and she begins to pant. "I'd do anything for you, anything."

"I know," she says, leaning down to kiss my lips. And then she starts rocking the way we both like it. The soft way. The easy way. The way that says we are in love. Her hands clasp together behind my neck as her tongue seeks out mine. I think I love the kiss the most. Her kisses are long and slow. Her tongue isn't eager and penetrating. It's smooth and moves to the rhythm of our bodies.

Fuck.

We come together a few seconds later. We are so in tune, so much alike in our wants and needs, so perfect.

"I know you love me, Ronin. And you love our daughters too."

"I do," I say, letting her cling to me in a way that reminds me of long ago. When we were scared and desperate. When things were unstable and dramatic.

"And that's why I know that you will not overreact when I tell you that Sparrow got a job offer to model for an equestrian magazine and I already told her she could do it."

3

FORD

"Get on your knees," I say. Ashleigh is wearing that black bra and panty set that I love so much. It's a signal we've had over the years. Oh, the lingerie is new. I gave it to her last night as a hint of what I've been craving. I do every once in a while when the sex gets too normal, just to spice things up. And if she puts it on, I know she's in the mood.

She put it on when she came back to bed from helping Ronnie with her baby.

God, I love her.

Ashleigh kneels down in front of me, her eyes trained on mine. I'm sitting on the bed wearing black silk pajama pants and I've been hard since I realized she was up for some fun. She puts her hands on my thighs, her palms down. Just the warmth from her touch makes me impatient. We don't do this a lot. Kids, work, dogs... these things have been interfering with our sex life for the last fifteen years. But Kate is sixteen and Five is fifteen, so their needs have become less time-consuming.

We've had lots of spare time lately.

"What do you want to do this time?" I ask her. "Spankings?" I waggle my eyebrows at her.

"Um…" She hesitates. "Maybe."

"Hmmm. You're not excited about it?"

"Well, whatever you want is fine."

"Fine? Since when do we use the word 'fine' to describe sex?"

"Well, I was just thinking—"

"Don't kneel then, Ashleigh. If you've got something on your mind I don't want to be looking at you on your knees." I pull her up and place her on the bed next to me. "Just tell me. You have something else in mind?"

"Well," she says, climbing in my lap and placing her hands on my shoulders. "I don't know if I need all that exciting stuff anymore. You know? I just like being near you, Ford. We can have sex any way you want and I'm happy. Just the thought of climbing into bed with you gets me excited."

"So you don't want the kinky shit right now?" I'm kind of confused. She put the lingerie on. That's the signal. But if she wasn't thinking about sex, then she must want something else.

I slip my hands behind her neck and pull her close so we can kiss. Her mouth is soft and her lips are plump against mine. I want to bite them so bad.

"I like the spankings. We can do that if you want."

"Hmmm," I say. "But it's not on the top of your list?"

She shrugs.

"Well, that's no fun, Ash. What kind of sex do you want then?"

"I don't want sex today. I want love."

Awww. "I can do love, love." My fingers slip under the silky bra strap and slide it down her shoulder. Her skin still prickles with anticipation when I touch her. Every single time. "You want slow, huh?"

"Yes," she whispers.

"You want tender?"

"Yes," she giggles. "I want slow and tender." Her hand slips down my shoulder, dipping and rising along the curve of my biceps. Her nails dig into my skin and I grow harder just at the thought of making her feel loved.

"Should we go on a date today?" I ask, sliding the other bra strap down so her full breasts begin to spill out of the cups. I squeeze them gently and kiss her mouth. "Should we take a ride on the gondola for old times' sake? Or get a room at the Travel Saver Motel and fuck like teenagers?"

She nips my lip as I talk and then her tongue slides in. "Maybe."

"Should we go eat at the diner and risk bumping into people who will tell you about my atrocious childhood?"

"That's an idea."

"Should we say fuck everyone and get on the road and drive to Vegas so we can hold hands in the aquarium?"

"That was the best week of my life," she sighs, pulling back a little.

"Me too. I mean, we've had a lot of great weeks, but that week was so special."

"Sometimes I wish we could go back, you know? Back to the beginning and redo all those things that brought us together."

"I don't need to go back to feel that way, Ashleigh. I like our present. I like you, and the kids, and the house, and the jobs, and everything. It's all perfect. Why go back and start again?"

"I don't know," she says. But she's sad for some reason, I can tell.

"What's on your mind?"

She pauses, looking me in the eyes. Her mouth opens like she has something to say, but whatever it was that was going to come out stays put. Something else comes out. "I'm not sure."

It's a lie. I can see right through her like she's glass. But I'm not pushy and Ashleigh knows how to talk about things. She's a psychologist. She knows what she wants to say, she's just not sure how to say it yet. So I just give her time. This is how we do things. We give each other time to think before we talk. There are no fights in our house. There's no drama, or yelling, or name calling. We are very careful with each other.

So I let it go until she's ready and pull her bra down to release her breasts. I squeeze them a little harder and she sucks in a breath of air. But at the same time, her hand reaches down and she wraps her fingers around the bulge in my pants.

It's my turn to suck in a breath. Even after all these years one touch is all it takes. I stand up, holding her to my chest as she wraps her legs around me. I place her on the bed and crawl up next to her body, stopping when my knees are on either side of her hips.

"Do I bore you?" I tease.

"Never," she says through her smile. "You are the farthest thing from boring, Mr. Aston."

"Mmmm," I growl as I unhook the front-closing clasp on her bra and slide it down her arms. Her breasts are still perfect. I lean down and bring one nipple to my mouth, sucking on it and kneading it at the same time. Her head tilts back and her hands clasp around my neck, her fingertips threading their way up into my hair.

I place my body over hers, rubbing my dick against her belly, and then reach down and slide her panties aside so I can slip a finger into a pool of wetness. Fuck. She turns me on. I ease back and hook my thumbs underneath the elastic, and then move off her legs so she can lift her knees and slip them down her legs. She bunches them up in her little fist and throws them across the room.

"Now you," she says, giving me a little wink.

I chuckle as I get off the bed and stand, then let my pants drop to the floor. Her eyes never leave my cock and that shit turns me on so bad. I wrap my hand around my shaft and pump myself a few times, eager to be inside her.

"Slow and tender?" I ask.

She nods. "Yes. I want it like that right now. I just need the love."

Why? I wonder if I've been missing some signals lately and that's why she feels needy. I hate the very idea. But she doesn't want to talk right now, I can tell. So instead of asking her, I kneel back down on the bed and place my body over hers. My arms are on either side of her head and I slip my fingers into her hair as I kiss her mouth. She responds by dragging her fingernails down my back in a way that makes every touch receptor fire in my skin.

I close my eyes, that's how much I like slow and tender Ashleigh this morning.

I lift my hips as she opens her legs, letting my cock find the pool of wetness. And then I ease inside her and she lifts her knees up, allowing me to push deeper.

"God, I love how you feel," I say.

"I love how you make me feel," she says back.

We get our rhythm going. And it's slow, just like she wanted it. It's better than having her on her knees looking up at me from the floor, that's for sure. It's so much better than giving her spankings or binding her wrists.

I like all that. And even though it's fun and sexy, this is so much more.

This is love.

I open my eyes and kiss her as we move, her lips fitting perfectly against mine. I hike one of her legs up towards her shoulder and turn her on her side a little, letting me hit that spot that makes her come as I rock against her. One of her hands squeezes a breast while the other slides down her belly and begins to rub her clit in small circles.

She drives me crazy when she does that. She knows she drives me crazy. Especially when her eyes are open when I fuck her.

"Ashleigh," I moan, pumping her harder because I want to come and then flip her over and do it again from behind.

"Ford," she says, arching her back, on the verge of release. "Ford," she says again.

Just the sound of my name coming out of her mouth is enough to push me over the edge.

I come inside her, squeezing her calf as I hold her leg up.

She moans out that seductive moan that has been driving me crazy for years and lets go at the same time.

I release her leg and lie down next to her, pulling her up to my chest, gently kissing her shoulder. "I will never get tired of this. Ever. Each year it gets better and better, Ashleigh. Each year I love you more and more."

"We've built a great life, Ford. I'm so happy I met you out on that freeway fifteen years ago. And I'd love to go to the diner today. And take a ride on the gondola. I'd love to relive it all again. Go back to the beginning and remember."

"And give up the mansion for the Travel Saver too?" I ask, smiling as I kiss her shoulder again.

"I liked back then when the kids were small and things were new. I liked it. So I'd love to relive that time in our lives, but I told Veronica I'd help her with dinner and baking."

I am just about to close my eyes and take a post-sex nap when she says this. I hear all her words, but the only ones that matter are *new again*. We've had this conversation before. A few times at least over the years. And it only ever went one place. Children.

She wants another baby.

4

SPENCER

"Hey, Ronnie?" I ask, little Cindy fussing in my arms. "Rons? I think she needs some more medicine for her teeth. Should we give her more medicine? It's been like eight hours."

"I just gave her some three hours ago, Spencer. You'll have to—" She sighs, then drags herself into a sitting position in bed. "Never mind, I'll do it."

"No," I say, stepping back as she reaches for Cindy. "I got it. I'm not new at this, I just needed to ask so I didn't give her too much." Cindy wriggles in my arms. She's been the crankiest of all the kids, and it figures, right? The early ones were easy. Ronnie had all kinds of energy with Rory and Belle. Jasmine and Ariel were a little tougher because when you've got a few kids it's hard to keep up. And when you have six, well, yeah, that shit gets downright challenging.

"Maybe…" Ronnie rubs her temples and closes her eyes. She's so damn tired. "Maybe go get that frozen teething ring from the freezer downstairs." She opens her eyes again and looks up at me. "I can get it."

"I got this, Veronica. Just go to sleep. You were up half the night. Cindy and I can kick it today. Ford's gonna take all the kids skiing, so you don't have to do anything but rest."

"I have to get dinner started."

"Stop," I say. "It's seven in the morning. Whatever you're cooking doesn't take ten hours."

"I wanted to make cookies…" She looks down as she places a hand over her stomach and then scowls. "But the last thing I need is cookies, so maybe it's better if I just skip it this year?"

"What?" Did she just body-shame herself? "You really need some sleep, Bombshell. Pronto. Go back to bed and I'll take care of things."

She doesn't even fight me, just drops her head back to the pillow and lets out a long sigh.

I ease out of the room quietly and take the baby downstairs. The house is big and the kitchen is far, but I can hear the bustle of kids and dogs before I even make it downstairs. When I walk in, it's a madhouse.

I love this fucking madhouse. My girls are all laughing and talking a mile a minute. Belle is stuffing her face with pancakes, Jasmine and Ariel are clinking their OJ glasses together like they are having a secret toast, and Rory is…

I squint my eyes at Rory. She's talking to Five, but that's not what makes me squint my eyes. She's wearing a Shrike Trikes t-shirt and sweat pants, but it's the way... it's the shape of her...

"Daddy," Rory squeals, getting up from her stool at the breakfast bar and coming towards me. "Five wants to know—"

"Absolutely not."

She stops short. "What?" Her smile falters.

Cindy smacks her little fist into my eyeball, and I have to take a deep breath. "I'm sorry, what were you going to ask?" I eye Five suspiciously. I know he's always liked her, but he's so weird. Like Ford, just weird. Always wearing those suits. Always on that computer. And he's been in and out of different college programs since he was ten or eleven. He's gone a lot and that's the way I like it.

But today he looks... different. Different in the same way that Rory looks different in her innocent nightclothes. He almost looks normal in his flannel pajama pants and Shrike t-shirt. Add in the fact that his normally perfectly coiffed hair is messed up a little like he just rolled out of bed, and I get flushed with anger.

In fact, Rory's long blonde hair is all messed up too. Flowing over her shoulders like an unruly waterfall. And Five is looking at her the way I look at the Bomb.

"But Daddy," Rory pleads. "I need to go shopping."

"Shopping?" I ask, ratcheting down my suspicions and getting a hold of my paranoia as the seconds tick off.

"Yeah, we don't want to ski today. We want to go shopping in the Village."

Shopping. I mull it over in my head. Lots of people there. Crowds of people, actually. Not private, in other words. "Maybe," I say. "But I'm pretty sure Ford is counting on you to help him, Five."

"Mr. Shrike," Five starts. "I've already cleared it with my father. Kate's helping him today. Right, Kate?" He looks over at his sister and there's… there's some kind of secret look going on between the two of them.

"Yup," Kate says. She is as normal as Five is strange. And she's been Ford's little sidekick since day one. But she's smarter than people give her credit for. I think she secretly likes it that way. Like being underestimated is the best gift she ever got out of being Ford's adopted daughter. "Ford and I are skiing a double black once the kids are finished."

"Well," I say, eyeing my brood. Rory needs a chaperone. Belle, Jas and Ariel won't go shopping. They love Ford too much to skip out on a whole day with him on the slopes. And there's no chance in hell that Rook and Ronin will have time to shop today. Sparrow has ballet rehearsal before *The Nutcracker* tonight. "Oliver," I say, smiling. "Ollie, my boy. You don't want to ski today, do you? You hate skiing." He does too, he can't ski worth a shit. "Will you go with Rory and finds something extra-special pretty for Mommy today? She's tired and needs a pick-me-up present before Santa comes."

"Yay!" Oliver says. "Yes, yes, yes! I want to go shopping with Five. He's the best, Daddy."

I roll my eyes. "OK, good. You can go, Princess, but…" I look at Five. "But…"

"But what, Daddy?" Rory asks.

But what am I going to say to Five? *You touch my girl, I'll break your fingers? I'll grab that shotgun I'm hiding under my bed and*—"Just be home in time for dinner. Your mom is making something special tonight."

"She says she's making healthy stuff tonight," Belle says, wrinkling her nose.

"Healthy stuff?" I have to shake my head at that one.

"Yeah," Jas pipes in. "She says she needs to go on a diet because her old jeans don't fit anymore."

"Diet?" I'm not following. The Bombshell has never looked so good in her life. God, her fucking tits, man. Every time I look at them, I want to fuck her.

"We don't want healthy food on Christmas Eve, Daddy," Rory says. And that's when it all becomes clear. The reason my princess looks so… different in her t-shirt are those… Jesus fuck.

My sweet little princess has turned into my Bombshell.

I stand there dumbstruck as the novelty of the bustling kitchen wears off and Cindy begins to wriggle in my arms again.

I absently find the teething ring in the freezer and hold it out for Cindy until her little hands are able to grasp it and fling her towards her mouth. She starts biting on it eagerly.

"You OK, Dad?" Oliver asks a few minutes later when

the kids are all back to their normal kid things and ignoring me.

I let out a long breath of air and lean down to whisper in Ollie's ear. "I'll give you twenty bucks and a ride on my motorcycle when we get back home if you tell me everything Five says to Rory while they are out shopping."

Oliver's face lights up. "Deal."

FIVE

Rory is dressed and ready and waiting downstairs before me. Hmmm, maybe Kate is right. Do I spend too much time on grooming?

"We're going to have so much fun today, Five!" Oliver says as he bounds down the steps ahead of me.

"Finally!" Princess says with a giggle. "I've been ready for twenty minutes."

"Where is everyone?"

"They all left. It's just us. Well, my mom is sleeping and your mom is making cookie dough for the decorating party after the ballet. I think my mom is stressed, Five. My dad said we should get her something special for Christmas while we shop, but she's not the kind of person who likes expensive trinkets, and that's all they sell in the Village."

"Yeah," I say back, mulling this over. "She does deserve something nice. She always cooks for us. And she throws the best birthday parties. What kind of things does she like? Maybe we can take the limo and go somewhere else?"

Rory's eye open wide. "The limo?"

"Let's take the limo. Let's take the limo," Oliver starts chanting.

"Will your mom let us?" Rory asks, her hopes high.

Now this is a way to make an impression, am I right? Taking your princess out in a limo for a festive day of Christmas shopping. "Let's go ask."

The three of us walk into the kitchen where Ashleigh— I'm allowed to call her Ashleigh in my thoughts—is busily banging baking sheets and grabbing mixing bowls from the cupboards.

"Hey, Mom, can we take the limo shopping? We want to buy Ronnie—"

"Aunt Ronnie," Ashleigh corrects me, as she searches through a drawer looking for something.

I roll my eyes. "—Aunt Ronnie a special present."

"Yeah," Rory chimes in. "And she won't think some over-priced gift from the Village is special. It says last-minute, Aunt Ash."

"That's true," I say, pointing a finger at Princess. "She works so hard, Mom. She needs a special present."

Ashleigh stops what she's doing, immediately suspicious of my intentions. I shoot her my innocent smile, but that only makes her scowl.

"My dad says do it up right, Aunt Ash. I feel we need to expand our horizons to find the perfect gift."

"Hmmm," Ashleigh says, thinking this over. "You're

right. She's sorta down today. And she was up all night with Cindy, so she's exhausted. Where do you think you're going to go?"

"There's an antique store in Copper," Rory says, her hands pressed together like she's begging and her little feet jumping up and down a little. "We could find something really cool there, I know it."

My mom frowns. "Copper Mountain?" She tasks her tongue. "I don't know."

"Oh, come on, Ashleigh." I do that on purpose to make her take us seriously. She trains her eyes on me, ready to pick a fight about what you call adults. But I hold a hand up. "We're not kids. It's not snowing. There's no ice on the roads. It's a limo, and Richard has been our Vail driver for ten years."

"He's not on call today, Five. It's Christmas Eve. So no. You kids will have to find something nice for her in town." And then she turns her back and returns her attention to the baking.

We walk back out to the foyer and when we get there, Rory has a royal pout on her face. "We're never going to find anything good, Five."

"I know!" Oliver says. "We can get her a new stroller for Cindy."

I shoot him a look.

"Don't be stupid, Oliver," Rory says. "She's tired of babies. She's got six kids. She doesn't want a new stroller. She wants something cool that makes her feel special and pretty. Like some new Frye boots. Or tickets to see

Metallica. Or a new leather jacket. Or..." Her words trail off but her eyes light up. "Oh my God, I have the best idea." But then her face falls again. "But it's back at my dad's shop."

"What is it?" I ask.

"Never mind," she says, clicking her tongue. "It's pointless to even talk about it, because we can't go all the way home."

"Hmmmm," I say.

"I know that hmmm," Oliver says. "It says Five has an evil plan." He rubs his hands together like a mad scientist.

"What if I can get us to Fort Collins? Do you know exactly where it is?"

Princess crinkles her face at me. "How would we get back to FoCo? It's two hours away."

"Well, we don't technically have to be back here until six for dinner. And it's only eight-thirty in the morning now. So we have tons of time."

She smiles a smile that matches Oliver's mad-scientist palm-rubbing. "Tell me."

"We can Uber." I smile as I say it. Uber is the teenager's gift from God.

"Won't Ash and Ford get an alert if we use the app?"

"Pffft. What do you think I am? A child? I've had my own credit cards since I was eleven."

My princess hooks her arm into mine and leans her head on my shoulder. "You're my hero, Five."

Wow. Life lesson learned. Find a way to give a woman what she wants and you turn into her hero.

"Come on," I say. "Let's walk down to the Village and call from there. I bet there are a ton of cars today."

"Will they take us all the way to Fort Collins?" Rory asks.

"They will if we pay them enough." That's one lesson I learned growing up Aston. Money talks.

6

RONIN

"I don't get why you're giving me the silent treatment," I say as we drive Sparrow over to the Vail theatre for the last *Nutcracker* dress rehearsal before the performance tonight.

"Sparrow," Rook says, an edge to her voice. "Do you want me to hang out with you backstage and do your hair and make-up?"

"Oh, yeah," she says. I look at my thirteen-year-old daughter in the rearview and smile. She's so perfect. Her dark hair, her blue eyes. They are the same blue as Rook's. The same blue as mine. Electric.

But I don't like the idea of modeling. Rook knows this. I'm the one who should be giving her the silent treatment for telling Sparrow yes before we talked it over. Once, when Sparrow was six and Starling was just a new baby, Antoine took pictures of them. And since they both have bird names, like Rook, Elise thought it would be cool to dress them up in feathers and make them look like birds.

Sparrow was holding Starling in her arms, her long dark hair falling over her face as she leaned down to give her new baby sister a kiss.

It was the most beautiful picture I've ever seen.

But lots of other people felt the same way. Antoine had it up in his office and every time a client came, they asked about it.

They asked about Sparrow, specifically. Was she available?

Was she fucking available? Antoine's photographs are more child-friendly these days—he mostly does fashion now. But back then he had a few lingering clients for the erotic stuff.

I saw red.

Normally I'm a pretty easy-going guy. I don't get worked up and I take it all in stride, knowing that there is a solution for every problem. But I punched that guy in the teeth that day. I almost got arrested. Antoine had to smooth things over so the client didn't press charges. Antoine ended up doing the shoot for free.

I do not want my daughter's face plastered all over the world like mine was. I do not want people to look at her and remark on her weight, or her legs, or whether or not she's graceful or she can hold a pose that reminds people of a cat. It's no one's damn business.

Rook knows this. She was there that day.

I huff out a breath.

And yet here I sit getting the silent treatment.

I pull into the Vail theatre and stop at the backstage

security guard and flash our pass. He nods at Sparrow, who looks like a dancer, even when she's not in her costume or leotard.

"Do you want me to come in too, Sparrow?" I ask her, smiling into the rearview mirror.

"We got this," Rook says, grabbing her purse. Sparrow is already halfway out of the backseat, pulling her bag filled with shoes, make-up and whatever else they use to put on a show behind her.

I grab Rook's hand before she can make her own escape and pull her close. "Why are you mad at me? I never said a word. I should be the one mad at you."

She crosses her arms. "Are you mad at me?" she challenges.

"No, but you know I don't like the idea of her modeling. I hate the thought of people looking at her."

"You do realize she's a ballerina, right? You do realize that there will be three hundred people watching her tonight?"

"It's not the same," I say, weary of this fight before it even starts. "It's dancing."

"It's the same thing. They want tall, skinny girls to dance, Ronin. They want girls who can work hard and dedicate their lives to the art. It's the same thing. So I don't understand why she can't model for this equestrian catalog."

"Well, you already told her she could, Rook. So if I say no, then I'm the bad guy."

"That's not the point. I want you to be happy for her.

She doesn't want to be a model, Ronin. She doesn't even want to be a ballerina. She wants to be a veterinarian. But along the way she wants to explore these other things. She loves riding. The job isn't about the modeling, it's about the location where they're doing the shoot. A big horse park down in Parker where she dreams of show jumping one day. And while we're on that topic, you complain about *that* too."

"It's dangerous."

"Well, why don't we just forbid Starling from skiing then? That's dangerous. Hell, let's just stop them from walking across the street when we get home. They might get hit by a car."

"There's risks, and then there's risks. Starling out on the bunny hill with Ford is—"

"Bunny hill?" Rook laughs. "Are you kidding me? When's the last time you went out there to see her ski?"

I sigh. I'm totally losing this battle. Because everything she said was true.

Rook opens her door and starts to get out, but then turns back. "I want you to enjoy them, Ronin. I want you to enjoy the skiing, the catalog shoot, the show tonight. The jumping she may or may not do next year. Because these kids are all growing up way too fast, and you're going to miss out on memories if you don't stop and enjoy it."

Rook gets out and closes the door, walking to the backstage door where Sparrow is waiting. I wave at them. Only Sparrow waves back.

Hmmm. Am I working too much? Is that what's she

saying? And what kind of skiing is Starling doing? I really don't go out on the slopes much. I'm busy running the Fort Collins theatre and we have film festivals twice a year. The prep work is never-ending. As soon as one festival ends, it's time to get ready for the next one. Six months is barely enough time to make it come off without a hitch. To make it perfection.

But I'm home every night for dinner. I do go see Sparrow ride because she takes lessons out at Spencer's farm with Kate and Rory and Belle. And I catch all her shows and recitals.

But Starling... she might get the short end of the deal from me. She's only six, so I guess I just figured she was too young to miss me at all her little kiddie activities. Soccer, and T-ball, and tennis.

Hmmm.

A car honks behind me and I wave to the eager stage parent who needs to drop off a daughter for rehearsal and ease the car forward.

I'm going to see what Starling is really up to out on those slopes.

7

FORD

"Here, Dad," Kate says. "Let me put this on you."

"What's that?" I ask, not taking my eyes off Starling as she navigates the freestyle area of the terrain park.

"Just a colored armband so the kids can find you easily."

"What?" I ask, looking down at the swath of red fabric. "Why do I need this? We only have Belle, Ariel, Jasmine, and Starling out here today."

"It's crowded, Dad," Kate says, looking down at a clipboard.

"Why do you have a clipboard?"

"Hey," a guy says next to me. "That's your kid right there?" He's pointing to Starling.

"Nah, my buddy's kid."

"How old is she?"

"Ummm…" I have to look at Kate for this.

"Six." Kate laughs.

"She's good."

"Yeah," I say, leaning back on my heels a little. "I've been coaching her since she was three. She's a natural." I look over at the guy. "My kids ski too." I nod at Kate, who is busy talking to a group of other kiddie skiers. "But it's not their love, you know? Starling loves it." God, I love that about her.

"Does she compete?"

"Oh, hell yes. I make her mother put her in every competition they have out here." Rook loves that Starling is a skier and she told me to spare no expense making her happy on the slopes. I secretly think she's doing it for me as much as for Starling. Ash and I have skied a lot since the kids were born. Nothing serious. But ever since Rook decided Starling needed ski lessons, I've gotten my passion back. I can see myself in this little girl. So much.

"What do you think about my kid?" the guys asks. "He's the one in the black and red."

"Ah," I say. "I've been watching him since he got here. He's good. How old is he?"

"Thirteen."

"Perfect age," I say.

"For?"

"Oh, you know. This is the perfect time to let him loose. Just let him do his thing. When I was his age I was up here every weekend in the winter. You guys local?"

"Denver."

"Yeah, that was us too. But my parents had a house up here, so we came as much as we could."

"He's totally into it." We watch the boy do some aerials.

A three-sixty, then a switch and grab. "I just fired his coach. That guy was so unreliable. Never even showed up at the last competition down in Loveland."

"Really?" I ask, looking back to Starling. I told her I'd take her on the terrain park after she warms up and we're just about ready.

"Yeah, so I'm glad I ran into you guys."

"What?"

"Um…" Kate is suddenly next to me with her clipboard. "Dad, this is Mr. Shalons. His son is Randy. And he's signed up for…" She clears her throat. "Two hours today."

"Right, two hours," the boy's father says wistfully. "I know your daughter said it was a one-time thing. But if you guys are local, then I'm interested, Mr. Aston."

"Interested in what?" I give the guy a classic sidelong Ford glance.

"Regular lessons. I'll pay, man. I know you're a busy guy, you have no time for my kid's dream and all that. But I've heard a lot about you."

"Like what?" I ask, my mood going sour fast. I have a long history of criminal activity. It's well behind me now, but it only takes one reminder to wipe away all the amnesia people have around here.

"Oh, you know, your shows. Spencer Shrike. You're a benefactor for that film festival up in Fort Collins."

"You've done some research."

"Hey, Mr. Aston," another kid calls, skiing up to me. He's about fifteen, same age as Five. "I'm ready to go, man. So stoked about this opportunity."

"What?"

"Dad," Kate says, checking off another name on her clipboard. "This is Josh Pittan. He won the Fancy Freestyle last weekend up in Breckenridge."

"Congrats," I say. "But—"

"He's here for four hours."

"Four? Hours?" What the hell is happening?

Two more kids ski up. "We're here!" they say, looking like brother and sister. "Sorry we're late, Mr. Aston. My mom couldn't get the car started this morning."

"She had to call us a cab," the sister says. "This is the best Christmas present ever!"

I shoot Kate a look. "Can you excuse us for a moment?" I tell the crowd. "I need a word with my assistant. Starling," I yell, just as she's about to pass me and give the moguls a try. "Hold up for a second."

"Safety first," the parent of the first boy says. "I like that."

"Kate, what the hell is going on?" I ask, after we ski off a little way. "Why do all these people think I'm running a class here today?"

She laughs. "You are, Dad. I set it all up."

I rub my face. "Why would you do that?"

"I heard you telling Mom that story about your Bronco last month when you guys were talking about the old days. You said you ran tours at the science museum to save up for a car. And I want a Bronco too. So I started a ski class."

"You can't start a ski class."

"Yeah, I can." She smiles sweetly at me. "It's

entrepreneurial. You love that. Plus, you let Five start that app stuff. It's only fair."

"But you're not teaching the class."

"Duh." She snorts. "I'm not that good. But you are. And you love skiing. And," she stresses the word, "you love teaching Starling. All these kids are good. Like really good," she says, lowering her chin. "I screened them all so you didn't get any lazy ones from tourists looking for a babysitter. They're all freestyle skiers and they've all won competitions."

I take a deep breath. "You can't make enough to buy a car with one day of classes."

"How do you know?" She smirks.

"How much did you charge?"

"Three-fifty an hour."

"What?" I look back at the parents and the kids. They all smile at me. "How much for today?"

"Three thousand, five hundred dollars."

"*What?*"

"How much do Broncos go for? Not the really tricked-out ones. One like yours?"

I scrub my hand down my face again.

"Daddy?" Kate asks sweetly.

"Katie," I say back. And then a laugh leaks out. "You're sneaky."

"I take after you."

"Jesus Christ."

"Did you know that Grandma called and asked if we were going to meet her at church tonight and I said we can't because we'll all be too tired after we watch Sparrow dance *The Nutcracker?*"

I forget about the kids for a moment and picture myself being forced to sit still in church tonight with my mother. She's up here with Gary, staying at the Four Seasons until we all drive home tomorrow for Christmas dinner. "What'd she say?"

"She said she totally understands. And she'll put in a good word for us when she and Gary go."

Whew. Dodged a bullet there. "OK, look. I'll do the class. I don't have much choice. But I'm not doing lessons. I'm not a ski coach, for fuc—Christ's sake."

"Got it, Daddy," Kate says, leaning up to give me a kiss on the cheek. She's about to ski back to the waiting class, but she stops and give me a long once-over. "But you could be, Daddy. You *could* be."

8

SPENCER

Cindy and I end up in the library. It's a lonely room at the very western edge of the house and it's nothing but floor-to-ceiling shelves filled with books. It even has one of those library ladders and a set of antique leather couches that are situated in front of a fireplace that is almost as massive as the one out in the main living room.

Cindy squirms in my arms until I place her the right way against my chest. She likes to rest her head on my shoulder, and she likes her little butt to be held up by my forearm.

When Ford, Ronin, and I decided we'd like to get a family house up here so we could vacation together with plenty of room as our families grew larger, we lucked out when this monstrosity came on the market. It's the oldest mansion in Vail, built by one of the town's founding developers. It has never been owned by anyone outside of that family since it was built in the early Sixties when the Vail resort was founded.

I never knew any of this shit about Vail. But Ford is like some sort of ski resort savant, and when he saw that the owners were selling everything in the library as part of the house—they added on seventy-two thousand dollars to the price tag, saying it was a treasure trove of historical documents they wanted to be preserved with the structure, so don't go thinking they were being generous—he bought the place without even asking Ronin and me.

But hell, it's a nice fucking house. Eight thousand square feet of luxury mountain home. Seven stone fireplaces, indoor and outdoor pools, almost two acres of land. That alone is worth the price. Gated, stable for the ponies we bring in the summer, and ski-in ski-out.

I can't complain about the house.

Hell, I can't complain about anything. I live a charmed life.

But my Bombshell might be sad. It might be the leftover hormones from the last pregnancy. But it might also be that I don't give her enough attention.

Do I work too much? Does she miss me? Do I not help out enough at home? Do we need more vacation time?

I look down at Cindy, who is momentarily content with the smooth rocking motion I'm doing as I look around the library. "What do you think, Baby Bomb?" I chuckle at that, until I realize the original Baby Bomb is turning into a full-blown Bombshell.

God. I'm not ready for my kids to grow up.

"At least I still have eighteen years with you, Cinderella. But you're definitely the last one. We've just about run out of princess names. I'm not sure Mulan Shrike works. And Pocahontas is just a no. Cindy Shrike, now that's damn cute, huh?"

She gives me a small smile and then her eyes go back to being droopy.

Well, Baby Bomb Five is just about content. Baby Bomb One, on the other hand. Whew. I'm not ready for boys. I'm really not. And Five Aston was never my pick. The whole princess thing he's been doing was cute when they were toddlers. Hell, it was cute when they were in Saint Joseph's together. But they're teenagers now. And Five is way too much like Ford for my comfort level. He's just about as tall as him. Same blondish hair, same light-brown eyes. Same freaky genius brain.

What if he's the same...

I have to shake my head to stop picturing Five with my Rory the way Ford used to be with his pets back before Ashleigh.

No. That's not going to happen.

And I'm so fucking lucky that Five is being sent all the way over to England for college in three weeks. I can accept a boy or two calling Rory on the phone. I can even accept dates after the football games she'll be cheering at for the next three years. But I cannot accept Five Aston as my Baby Bomb's long-term love interest.

It's not going to happen.

When I look back down at Cindy, she's sleeping. So I

walk out of the library and head to the kitchen. I'm not sure how much I want Cindy to sleep today. She's off her schedule, and that's why my Bombshell isn't getting enough rest at night.

"Hey, Ash," I say, walking into the family room that's open to the kitchen. "What's up in here?"

"Oh," she says, frowning and wiping her brow with her forearm. She leaves a streak of flour across her face. "Just finishing up the dough so the kids can decorate cookies tonight before bed."

We've been doing that since they were old enough to hold an airbrush. My kids decorate Christmas cookies like artists.

"I've only got a few more batches to make before I start the baking." And then she notices Cindy. This makes her whole face light up. "How's that little princess doing? Need some help, Spencer?"

I look back down at Cindy. "I think she's about out. But I don't want to put her to bed. I want her awake this morning so she'll nap later and be rested for the ballet tonight."

"You can put her down on the sectional. I'll watch her while she rests. And there's enough going on in here that she won't sleep too deeply."

"Hey, that's a good idea." Ashleigh has Christmas carols going, and the sound of the kitchen appliances should be enough to keep Cindy from sleeping too long.

"Why don't you leave her with me," Ash says, coming towards me with her arms out. "I don't get enough baby time these days." I hand over my little Bomb and Ashleigh takes her. She actually sighs as she brings Cindy to her chest.

Yeah. Ashleigh wants another kid. I've seen it coming for a couple months now. And Ford was never interested in having more after Five. He was so freaked out about passing on his... unusual genetics... they never had another one.

But Kate is sixteen now. She's driving and looking at colleges. And hell, Five skipped the teen years altogether and went straight to mini-adult several years back. It's gotta be tough to know that her mommy days are just about over.

"Do you mind if I go check on Ronnie?" I ask.

"Not at all, Spence. I got this." And then she smiles and takes Cindy over to the huge sectional couch we have set up in the family room.

"OK, text me if you need some relief."

"Take your time," she calls back as I make my way towards the front stairs.

When I enter the bedroom, it's dark. The drapes are still closed and there's nothing but Ronnie's soft breathing.

I look at her. God, she's so fucking beautiful. She's not even wearing anything special, just a pink nightie I got her a few years ago. But her blonde hair spills out onto the white pillowcase like she's been posed for a photoshoot. And her face is just as soft and pretty as I remember it back in college. I take my t-shirt off and slip in the bed next to her, wrapping my arms around her body and pulling her close.

She sighs, then turns to face me. Her eyes open slowly, but she doesn't smile.

"What's wrong, Bombshell?"

"I feel ugly," she whispers, not meeting my gaze.

"What?" I'm stunned.

"I can't lose these last twenty pounds, Spencer. I eat too much, I don't exercise enough, and none of my old jeans fit."

"Wait. You think you're fat?" I have to shake my head. "You can't be serious. You're perfect, Veronica Shrike. Perfect."

"I don't feel perfect, Spencer. I feel old. And ugly. And fat."

"Awww, baby. You need to take my word on this. I'm the boss and I say you're perfect. Come here," I say, pulling her even closer. "You turn me on so bad, Ronnie, all I have to do it look at you and I get hard. Feel." I place her hand over my cock, which is like stone, and then kiss her on the mouth, whispering, "You make me think dirty things, Veronica. All day, every day. All I think about is how much I love to fuck you."

"I don't feel like fucking."

Wow. I don't think I've ever heard her say that before.

"I just can't enjoy myself unless I feel sexy, Spencer. And I don't feel sexy."

"You are sexy, Ronnie. So fucking sexy. I lose my shit every time I look at you."

"I just want to lie here. Can we just lie here?"

I sigh. She's not in the mood to believe me. She's in the mood to pout and get her way. I can't stand the thought of it. I can't stand that she thinks she's not attractive anymore. It breaks my biker heart. So I just hold her tight and say, "Anything you want, Boss of Me. Anything you want."

9

FIVE

Our Uber car pulls into the Saint Joseph's parking lot just as a wedding party comes through the front doors and begins to congregate on the steps. We stop a little way off, so we don't disrupt their moment.

"Thanks," I tell the driver, as Oliver, Rory, and I get out. "Merry Christmas."

He Merry Chistmases me back and we slam our doors and he pulls out.

A giant shout goes up from the wedding party, and Rory starts walking towards them just as the bride comes through the doors. The bride's got her bouquet held up high, and then she throws it... right into the hands of my princess.

Rory laughs, and every bridesmaid turns to see who got lucky.

"Who is that?" they ask. So I quickly take Rory's hand and pull her along the sidewalk.

"Well," Rory laughs, "that's one way to start a day!" She beams down at the little bouquet of pink and white flowers.

"You know that means you're going to get married, right, Rory?" Oliver says, skipping a little to keep up with us. "It means you're next. It probably even means," Oliver continues, "that you'll marry Five, because he's your date today."

Rory laughs, and I almost choke. *Smooth move, Oliver,* I think. *There's no better way to scare a girl off than hinting at marriage on the first date.*

"I think Five is a pretty good catch, so that's cool with me."

"What?" I ask, instantly sorry I said it out loud.

"What?" Rory asks back. "I thought you've been in love with me your whole life, Five Aston? I thought you had our marriage all planned out back when you were seven?"

She likes me? Does this mean she really likes me? As more than the leader of the infamous Saint Joseph's Science Fair Rebellion back when she was nine?

"You know, I'm really going to miss you, Five."

"You are?"

"Why are you so surprised?" she asks. "We're like soulmates, right?"

"Right," I say back. "But your dad, and my school, and that football guy..."

"Football guy?" Rory asks. And then she shoots Oliver a look. "I'm not allowed to date, Five. My dad would seriously blow a blood vessel if I was dating."

"Yeah," I say, realizing I'm still holding her hand. Realizing she's still letting me. "Your dad hates me."

"He's just being a dad, Five. He has five daughters who will grow up to look like my mom. If you were him, you'd hate you too."

I laugh at that. "True. I have to give Spencer that one." I sigh. "I'm really going to miss you too. I feel like I've wasted the last year. Like once I leave, this whole thing we have will leave with me. That you'll just go on with your life and forget about me."

She gives my hand a squeeze. "Don't make me cry, Five. I don't want to think about that yet. You're not leaving for three more weeks and we have this whole day together. And we're far, far away from my dad right now. No one will see us. Let's forget about that and just have fun today."

"What should we do?" Oliver asks.

Shit, I forgot about the kid.

"I dunno. You decide, Five."

"Well," I say, my eyes darting around downtown Fort Collins. It's beautiful at Christmas. The main street shops are decked out with lights. There's a Santa Claus over there. Crowds of people are milling about, trying to get some last-minute gifts from the little shops that line College Avenue. And at night... Jesus, don't get me started. This place is magical when it's lit up at night. Then the smell of lunch at Anna Ameci's invades my senses, and I look across the street. "Let's get lunch first. Come on," I say, pulling her along. She grabs Oliver's hand and pulls him along too.

We cross the street and make our way towards the restaurant. Anna Ameci's is packed. They have a bakery in the back that you get to through the alley, but on Christmas Eve there are so many people lined up to get cookies and stuff, they take over the front too.

I keep a tight hold on Rory's hand and lead her and Oliver through the crowd until we reach the hostess.

"Hey, you guys," Rose Ameci says as we walk up. We've gone to school with her for as long as I can remember. "You here for lunch?"

"Yes," I say. "Table for three."

"I thought you guys go to Vail for Christmas?"

"We do," Oliver says. "But we're pulling a Ferris Bueller today."

I look down at Oliver. "What do you know about Ferris Bueller?"

"Ronin had an Eighties day at the theater last summer and he's been obsessed with Ferris ever since," Princess says. "You missed it. You were at college last summer."

I frown, but Rose laughs and says, "Well, I'll help you out and give you the works." She winks at me and I look over at Rory. Rose had a thing for me back in elementary school.

But Rory plays it cool and says, "Thanks, Rose. Five and I are celebrating our engagement today." She holds up her bouquet of flowers. "I caught it. Which means we're destined to be married."

I might blush at that.

She squeezes my hand again.

"They're gonna kiss tonight," Oliver says. "My dad is going to kill him afterward, but it will be worth it."

"Oliver," Rory squeals. But when she looks at me, her ears are a little pink.

God, my life would be complete if I could end this day with a kiss from Rory.

Rose gives us a huff for that last remark, but she does lead us over to the best table in the restaurant. It overlooks the street, and we have a full view of all the festive decorations and people in downtown.

I pull out Rory's chair and she sits, glancing up at me with a smile. Oliver takes the seat next to her and I sit across, so I never have to take my eyes off her as we start our first date.

"What else should we do with our day?" Oliver asks.

"What should we do, Five?" Rory asks, smiling that smile that has lit up my life for as long as I can remember. "Make it good," she says. "Make it count. Make me never forget it, so that when you leave me behind next month, I have this day to remember you by."

My heart hurts a little just thinking about leaving. I swallow hard. "We could go on a carriage ride around downtown." She loves horses.

"Yes," she whispers. "That's perfect."

"And then..." I rack my brain for more ideas on the perfect date. "And then we could go ice skating on the little rink they put near the Santa Claus house in the shopping district."

"I want to see Santa Claus!" Oliver squeals. "Can we stop and see Santa Claus?"

"Sure," I say, never taking my eyes off my princess. "And then we can stop at that art gallery they have on Mountain and College. I hear there's a new exhibit."

"I'd love that. My mom's been talking about it all week."

"And then we'll get that present for the Bomb and maybe it will be dark early tonight, and we'll get to see the lights come on?"

"I love the lights at Christmas," Rory says, her gaze wistfully redirecting to the decorations outside.

"Me too," Oliver says.

"It's going to be the perfect day, Five," Rory says, bringing her attention back to me.

"I'll make sure it is," I say back. And maybe, just maybe, we will have our first kiss. Maybe it will even be out under the lights. Maybe we'll stand right in front of the town Christmas tree.

Maybe.

RONIN

"What the hell is he doing?" I ask Kate as I ski up to her. I've been looking for them for over an hour. "And why the fuck didn't he text me back? I've been messaging him for like forty-five minutes." I stop and stare at Ford. "Is he…"

"Signing autographs," Kate answers, staring down at a clipboard. "Yup," she says with a small chuckle.

"Why?" I ask.

"Oh, he's running an advanced freestyle ski class today and we only had six spots for that. But I added a meet-and-greet to the Kickstarter."

"Wait a minute." I feel like I'm living in an alternate reality. "Ford has a Kickstarter? Why? That bastard has more millions hidden away than he can count."

"Oh, not for him." Kate finally gives me her attention. "For me. So I can make money to buy a car."

"And Ford was on board with this?" I can only shake my

head. "Is he drunk?" He better not be drunk when he's taking care of my kid.

"No." She laughs. "But he's enjoying it. And he could hardly say no when I told him how much money I raised. The kids are taking a break, so he's doing the meet-and-greet while they grab drinks. Starling is with—oh, there she is. Starling!" Kate yells. And then Star sees me and starts skiing over to us.

"Hey, Daddy!" she says, her cheeks bright red from the cold. "When did you get here?"

"Just now," I say, smiling down at her. "Are you having fun?"

"Yes. Are you going to stay and watch me?" She sips her hot chocolate.

"Absolutely. Your mom says you're doing some special stuff up here. I've been missing it, I guess. Sorry about that."

"That's OK," she says. "You're busy with work."

"Ronin," Ford says, skiing over to us after breaking away from his fans. I don't even know how to process that. "I didn't expect to see you here today."

"Yeah, well." I huff out some air, then look at Kate. "Rook says Starling is..." I have to stop talking because I don't know enough to even ask the right question.

"Kicking ass on the slopes?" Ford fills in. "You bet. You miss every competition. Did you realize that?"

"What? How did I not know she was competing?"

"I guess you take Sparrow to ballet on Saturdays?" Ford

shrugs. "But she's been in three so far this year. You didn't miss much last year."

"Wait, she competed *last* year?" No. That's not possible.

"Just little shit. I took her with me because even Rook was busy last winter. But this year, she's hardcore, Ronin. A little phenom. Anyway, my kids are back from their break. Starling is just hanging out with us for another two hours, then I'm going to take her down the terrain run and time her."

And then Ford skis off to 'his kids.'

I look down at Kate, but she's busy with her clipboard. So what can I do? I watch my daughter ski her little heart out while Ford barks orders at kids who eat up every word.

"He's a coach?"

"He is now," Kate says. "I knew he'd love it. But he'd never agree to it if I asked. He's too modest."

I almost choke.

"Every parent here has asked for private lessons. But we don't have time for that. We'll do groups, just like this. Oh," she says, looking down at her clipboard. "It's three-fifty an hour for Starling, but I'll give you a twenty percent family discount. That cool?"

I'm silent as I take all this in. And then I turn to look at Kate again. "Do you think I work too much?"

"Um..." She laughs. "Well, do you want the truth? Or do you want me to make you feel better?"

"The truth, Kate. Do you think I work too much?"

"Well, you never come to the slopes, but Rook doesn't

come either. And you do go to the horse shows. So that's a tick mark in your plus column."

"Are you doing that photoshoot for the equestrian catalog?"

"Oh, yeah."

"Ford's OK with that?"

"Why wouldn't he be?" she says absently, making a notation on her clipboard about a kid who goes flying by us.

"Well, it's modeling."

She shrugs. "We only want to do it for the horses, Ronin. Sparrow knew you'd hate it, that's why she only asked Rook."

"Rook told her yes."

"I know." Kate smiles up at me. God, when did she get so big? And she's only a few years older than Sparrow. Rook was right. I'm missing this shit. I'm missing out on their childhood. And we're not having any more kids, so this is it. Starling is six now, so it feels like I have such a long time to enjoy them later. But it feels like Sparrow was just turning six and now she's dancing in *The Nutcracker* and getting modeling offers, and talking about becoming a veterinarian.

How does the time fly by so fast?

I ponder that in mostly silence as I watch Kate watch the kids. I watch Starling too, but she's just messing around, waiting for Ford to be done so he can take her down that terrain run. I can ski, but I'm not great at it like Ford is. I manage, and really, I only come to the slopes to drink in the bar or hit the hot springs with Rook after we're done.

But fuck it. When all those kids are done and Starling is looking at Ford like he's the god of skiing, I suck it up and join them.

I fall on my ass, my face, twist an ankle going over the bars, try a three-sixty and eat snow, then a one-eighty and decide I should be wearing a helmet if I want to live through this little experiment.

But I realize something as we go down that hill over and over again, until the lights come on and I remember I have another daughter who wants my attention tonight.

I realize I've fucked up. I'm missing it. I work too much and play too little.

And I'm going to change that this year. I'm going to partake. I'm going to be invested. I'm going to enjoy it.

11

FORD

"Well?" Kate asks, as all the girls jump out of the car and run up to the house. "Did you have fun today, Daddy?"

I give her a sly look, but she shoots me one back. "You don't need to Daddy me, Duchess. I had fun."

"I knew it." She laughs. "I knew you'd enjoy it. So you're gonna give a few of them a spot in the regular class, right?"

"Hey, don't get ahead of yourself. I told them I'd consider it. And I will. But I need to talk it over with your mom. See what she thinks about this."

"Well, *I* think," Kate says as she opens her door and starts to get out of the car, "that you stopped producing shows last year because you're bored. So why not do this, Dad? These kids are good. You should make a documentary about them. About skiing. Do something artsy for a while, you know? Just relax a little and have fun."

She pauses after her little daughter speech and gives me a warm smile.

"Maybe, Katie. Maybe I will."

And then she nods and gets out, closing her door behind her.

But the door opens again and Ronin gets in. "Hey, man," Ronin says, rubbing his hands together to warm them up. "Do you think I work too much?"

"What?"

"Work too much. Rook thinks I work too much, and I have to admit, I never thought I did until she brought it up this morning. And then when I realized Starling was doing all this ski stuff, and I had no idea about any of it, it dawned on me that she might be right. Do you think I work too much?"

"We all work too much, Ronin. That's the kind of guys we are. Spencer would be at his shop seven days a week if he didn't have the garage at home to keep him busy. Your film festival is just starting to really gain international attention. And I took my family to New Zealand to film every January for almost a decade. We love our jobs, what can we say?"

"Yeah, but we live in town. I live four blocks from my work. And I had no idea Starling was so interested in skiing, let alone so good at it."

I shrug. "Do you want me to help you feel guilty, Ronin? Because I'd be more than happy to do that for you."

He ignores my dig. "And do you think I'm unreasonable about not wanting Sparrow to model? I mean, you saw my life. You saw what happened to Rook. What if Sparrow's good at it? What if they like her? What if she gets more jobs? She says she wants to be a veterinarian now, but what if those offers come in and she sees the fame, and the money, and the travel?"

"Hmm." I can see his point. In fact, I'm on his side on this. I don't mind Kate doing the shoot with Rory and Sparrow, but I know for certain Kate has no interest beyond the horses. She's so much like me, it's hard to remember I adopted her. She has a life plan. She's got her college all picked out. We've had interviews with them. Hell, she's been working for Ronin in the marketing department for the FoCo Film Festival for two years now. This modeling gig is what cheering at a football game is to Rory. It's what app development is to Five. It's the T-ball Starling does, and the riding lessons for Belle and Jasmine. Hobbies.

But Sparrow is strikingly beautiful. She is practically Rook's twin. If I were Ronin, I'd be worried too. She will be noticed the moment her headshot hits the agencies, if only for who she is. The niece of Antoine Chaput. The daughter of Ronin Flynn.

"Ford?" Ronin asks when I don't continue. "How do I handle it?"

"I think Rook wants to believe in Sparrow, Ronin. I think Rook knows the two of you started your adult lives the wrong way. You had a rough beginning and then Antoine was not exactly the typical American Dream, right? Erotic modeling? And Rook was married young and had all that drama she needed to get away from. Hell, all of us had unusual opportunities when we were teenagers and we made some bad decisions. So I think Rook looks at Sparrow as an opportunity to do it right. Let her have that. Maybe Sparrow becomes a model, but maybe all she wants is a chance to sit on a horse in thousand-dollar boots and get her picture in a catalog? You won't have a say in any of it in a few more years. Better to let her figure it out now than take a job when she's eighteen and unprepared."

He sighs again. "How did they grow up so fast?"

"God, I have no idea. But I've been thinking about it all day. Do you think Ashleigh wants another baby?"

Ronin laughs. "Only for like the past ten years."

"What?"

"You didn't notice?" He's grinning like the old Ronin, the one who has life by the horns and misses nothing. "Didn't you see the way she looked at Starling when she was born? And the way she looked at Oliver and Ariel. But you guys were the perfect family, right? One boy, one girl, that pack of dogs. What more could you ask for? I mean, Spencer was trying for a boy, but he just had one Princess Shrike after another."

We both laugh as we picture Spencer with all his little girls. Dressing them up in biker jackets and boots. Making them little Shrike Trikes for Christmas and birthdays. Teaching them how to change the oil while the cameras rolled for the TV show, or choose the right tailpipe for the design he was working on.

"I guess I should give Ash what she needs, right?" I look at Ronin.

He lets out a long breath and looks out the window. "I guess I need to do the same for Rook," he says back.

We get out of my car and walk up to the massive double front doors to the mansion. "Good talk, man," Ronin says as I pull one door open.

"Right, good talk."

We are accosted with the smell of food the second we enter, and then the noise, and my pack of face-eater dogs. Maybe I have so many dogs to take my mind off the children I was afraid to have?

The bustle of the families we've created over the years brings me out of my funk and I look around and enjoy it. Spencer is slow-dancing with Ronnie in front of the fireplace. Rook is lining cookies up on the long dining room table so the kids can decorate them like we do every Christmas Eve. And Ashleigh is standing in front of the fifteen-foot-tall Christmas tree, backlit by bright lights, watching me come into the fray.

I smile at her as I take off my coat and hang it over a chair in the foyer.

She shrugs, like she's apologizing for wanting something she shouldn't.

I walk over and take her hand, give it a kiss. "I missed you today, Mrs. Aston."

Her face crumples a little and she looks like she might cry. But she doesn't. She holds it together and leans up on her tiptoes in a way that reminds me of another mountain house, in what seems like another lifetime. "I have something to tell you," she whispers as she kisses my cheek.

I pull her into a hug, knowing full well what she wants to tell me. She's not done mothering. She's not ready for kids in college. She needs another baby. And she's afraid to tell me that because I was so worried about me, so worried about what sort of genetic contribution another child of mine might get, that I never once thought about what she was giving up to ease my concerns.

But we both stay silent and enjoy the peace we have. We just dance alongside Ronnie and Spence to *Silent Night*, our feet slow and our hearts full.

And then I glance up at Spencer and find a confused look on his face. "What's wrong?" I ask.

"Where the hell are Rory and Oliver?"

"Shit," Ashleigh says. "Fucking Five."

12

FIVE

I hold Rory's hand as Oliver finally gets his turn at Santa Claus. He's rattling off gifts like he's got a catalog in front of him.

"And I want a bike, just like my dad's," he says.

The Santa here in downtown FoCo is pretty realistic. Genuine white beard and everything. "Ho, ho, ho," Santa says. "What kind of bicycle does your daddy have, son?"

Oliver screws up his face. "Bicycle? My dad makes Shrike Bikes. I don't want a bicycle, I want a motorcycle! I want one with white skulls and black ravens. I want the tank to be scarlet red, just like the one my dad rides to work in the summer. I want leather seats and cool pegs. And I want a jacket to go with it. And tattoos, just like the ones my mommy drew on my dad. And I want—"

"Little boy, you can't have a motorcycle for Christmas! Ho, ho, ho!"

"What?" Oliver squeaks, like his dream is being crushed.

"Yes, I can. My dad made all the girls a Shrike Bike. Ask my sister!" He points to Rory and we get a stern look from Santa.

"Trikes," I correct Oliver. "He gives the kids Shrike *Trikes*. Not bikes."

"Yeah." Rory laughs. "Are you kidding? My dad wouldn't give us motorcycles!"

"Ho, ho, ho," Santa says again, setting Oliver down and shaking his head a little. "Well, a trike I might be able to manage. Now hurry along and don't forget to put out cookies for me tonight! Ho, ho, ho!"

Oliver shoots Santa a look, but reluctantly walks over to Rory and me. He lets off a huge sigh. "He wasn't even listening to me."

"Don't worry about it, Ollie," Rory says, taking his hand in her free one. "Santa can't afford a Shrike Bike. Only Daddy can give us Shrike presents. And I'm sure he's got something special for you under the tree."

"If it fits under the tree, then it's not a real Shrike Bike."

"Come on," I say. "It's almost dark. Let's go look at the lights before we have to get home."

"Yeah, what time is it? We need to go grab the present and Uber back to Vail soon," Rory says.

"Plenty of time," I tell her. It's already four thirty, so we're going to be late, but I don't care. I'm not ending our date until we have that perfect moment.

Now it's Rory's turn to sigh. She stops walking just as we reach the huge community Christmas tree and looks up at me with a smile. "This was the best day ever, Five."

It really was. Fantastic lunch at Anna Ameci's, ice skating—even though Oliver ate shit like six times and then wanted to stop. The carriage ride, window-shopping, and then the art gallery. We had to sneak by Sick Boyz, which was open until one today, to avoid all Rory's uncles. But they're closed down now, and we can enjoy the walk back over to the Shrike showroom where she insists she has the perfect present for her mom stashed away in the back of Spencer's office.

I look down at Rory. Her sapphire-blue eyes and her sweet, sweet face. She's the perfect girl for me. She's been the perfect girl for me since I laid eyes on her. And even though most of my thoughts growing up were about how to get her to join me in my delusional dreams of science fair domination at Saint Joseph's, the past year or so I've been starting to think of what we might become instead of what we already are.

We're friends now, but somewhere in the back of my head, I've always wanted to marry her. Even if it was just the little-kid version of marriage. And now I'm leaving. Just as we get to the age where we might start imagining about the more adult version of our relationship.

I'm going to lose her. I realize this. There is no way to make time stand still. There is no reasonable way to ask her to wait for me. There is no possibility of me not going to Oxford. And I don't even want to stay, either. I want her, but I want to start moving forward too. I've been holding myself back just to stick around. But I can't do it anymore.

We have to grow up some time.

"This was the best day of my life as well, Rory." I mean it too. And she knows I mean it.

She frowns a little, her face lit up by the brightly colored lights of the tree. "I'm gonna miss you so much, you know."

I nod. "I'm gonna miss you too."

"I know I play girl games with you. Pretending not to notice you looking at me. Or pretending not to look at you back. But Five, I've counted on you to be there for me my whole life. I cannot even imagine you leaving."

I feel a little sad all of a sudden. "I go away to school all the time, but I always come back, Rory."

She nods. "I know. But this is different. You were a kid. And you might only be fifteen, but you're not a kid anymore, Five. You're going to be thousands of miles away this time. There will be an ocean and so many time zones between us, we'll never even chat on the phone. We can't even text unless we figure out the time difference beforehand. It's going to be different. Everything is going to change."

"We can just..." I sigh now too. "We can just make a pact, you know? Like, we'll promise each other that we'll talk all the time. Make an effort."

"I don't want our friendship to be an effort. It's never been an effort before. You were just there. You were always just there. And now you won't be anymore. I'm going to be all alone."

"You have Sparrow. And Kate."

"I know." She looks up at me, her sapphire eyes watering like she might cry. "But I want you."

I pull her into a hug, wrapping my arms around her tightly. "Don't be sad, OK? I promise I'll be back for Spring Break. And all summer too."

She shakes her head as she buries her face in my coat. "You always do geeky stuff in the summer. You go to special places for geniuses and think about things that will change the world. You're going to meet people over there who are just like you, and you might even come back a few times, but then…" She looks up at me. "But then one day, you'll be like, I'm too busy to go home this time. I'm just going to stay. And that will be it for us, Five. We'll never recover from that. Because we're still kids right now, but we won't be kids forever. We're going to grow up."

God, she's so right. Everything she just said is right. And I'm not even sure there's a way to stop it. Life just… goes on. I want to make it better. Make her stop being sad and be happy. Make her smile again. I don't want her last memory of this day to be all the things we will regret in the future.

So I lean down. My heart beats faster. I lean down and she leans up, and we are so close. Our lips are so close.

"Rory?" A deep voice makes us pull apart unexpectedly. "Five? Oliver?" Vic Vaughn—Veronica's older, massive, built-like-a-monster, and tatted-up-in-scary-ways brother —is looming over us with a scowl on his face. "I thought you guys were in Vail for Christmas? What the hell are you doing down here in Fort Collins?"

SPENCER

SPENCER

"Don't glower at me," Ford says.

"I'm not glowering," I say back. But it comes off as defensive, and irritable, and glowering. "I'm just saying he should know better."

"Spencer," Ash says. "We'll talk to him, OK? He doesn't mean any harm and I'm sure they were never in danger or they'd have called. All of them know that we're on their side, no matter what happens, and they can call us for anything."

"That's not—" I soften my tone with Ashleigh. Not just because Ford won't tolerate me taking out my anger with Five on her, but because Ashleigh is a soft sort of woman and shouldn't be spoken to the way I started speaking to her. So I take a deep breath. "It's not that I think she's in danger, Ashleigh. It's that my daughter is fourteen, she looks like my wife, and I'm getting the urge to keep a shotgun on my person." I sigh. "If you get my drift." I catch a small chuckle from Veronica, which makes me stop and smile at her. It might be the first sign today that she's feeling better. "Right, Ronnie?"

She sighs heavily, reminding me that things are not OK. "I think they're fine. I think Five was wrong to take them so far away, but Five is Five. And his last name is Aston, so even if something did happen, he'd know what to do about it. I think Oliver probably had the time of his life and Rory finally got a chance to say what's on her mind. What's been on her mind for months now."

"What?" I ask. "What's on her mind?"

"OK," Ford says, looking at his phone. "I just got a text. They're getting off the freeway now and they'll be here in a few minutes. I'll talk to Five." With that Ford takes Ashleigh's hand and they walk out of the library and back to the party going on in the great room.

"Come on, Spencer," Ronnie says. "You know what's going on. Five is leaving in a few weeks and she's sad."

I scrunch up my brows. "Define sad."

"Sad," Ronnie stresses. "Like first crush, broken-hearted kind of sad."

"Sad like you," I say, not even meaning to.

She frowns so heavily, it makes me sad too. "I'm not really... sad, Spencer. I'm just feeling... undesirable. And tired. And this is new for me, you know?"

When she lifts her eyes up to meet mine, I see tears. "Ronnie," I say, crossing the few steps that separate us so I can bring her into a hug. "I fucking hate this. You're so goddamned desirable to me, it drives me crazy."

"I love being a mom, Spencer. You know I do. But six kids…" She shakes her head. "It changes a person. I feel lost. I feel like I don't even recognize myself anymore. I feel… old. And then Ashleigh is sad about not having any more babies, so that makes me feel ungrateful."

I hold her tight. I have all the words ready to say. All the words she needs to hear. But words might not be enough. "I love you. I know that's not what will fix the way you feel, but Veronica, I love you. And if I knew how to take this feeling away, I'd do it in a heartbeat."

"I know that, Spence." She sniffs away the tears and rests her head against my chest. "It's just a little setback. I just need to find myself again, that's all."

We hear the bustle of activity as Rory, Oliver, and Five come home and the dogs go crazy. Then the booming voice of Vic as he greets Ford and Ronin.

"I'll send Rory in so you can talk to her before dinner, Spencer. But don't be harsh. It's Christmas Eve and I just want everyone to be happy."

She tries to pull away, but I keep a tight hold. "That's all I want too, Veronica."

Her head tilts upward and she smiles. "I know." She pulls away and walks out, leaving the library door open behind her.

I turn to the windows and look out at the snow. It's just starting to fall, but the flakes are the big, heavy kind that pile up quick and make perfect snowballs for a fight.

"Daddy?" Rory says, a few minutes later.

"Close the door, Princess," I say, without turning around.

The door squeaks and then taps closed. "I'm sorry, Daddy. We shouldn't have gone off like that."

When I turn she's standing straight and tall, her head tipped up to look me in the eyes. Her long blonde hair is slightly wet from outside, the big heavy flakes nothing but spots of water now. She smiles.

I laugh.

"Really, Daddy. I'm sorry. But I'd like you to know..." She takes a deep, deep breath and a smile lights up her face. "I had the most perfect day with Five."

But just as quick as the smile appeared, it disappears. And then she looks just like Ronnie did a few minutes ago. Sad.

"What did you guys do?" I ask, waving her towards the couch and taking a seat. She follows, sitting down next to me.

"I caught a bouquet of flowers at a Saint Joseph's wedding, and we went to eat at Anna Ameci's, and then..."

She tells me about her whole day. Every last moment of it, right up to the part where she thought Five was going to kiss her as they stood in front of the city Christmas tree in downtown. She smiles for every second of her tale. Until that last part. She swallows hard and the silent tears stream down her face. "I always thought things would stay the same, you know?"

I know. I thought that too.

"I always thought that no matter what happened, Five

Aston was my knight. And all I had to do was press his face on my phone and he'd come rescue me. But he's not going to be here anymore, Dad. He's going to be so far away, he'll forget everything he loves about me before next summer."

I pull her into a big Daddy hug and hold her tight. "He won't, Princess. I promise. Five Aston is your forever guy. He's always going to be your knight, I promise."

"I want to believe it, Dad, but I just don't." She pulls away, sniffing just the way Veronica did. "I just don't have it in me to pretend that this is a fairy tale and love is magic. It's not. It's real life and he's leaving. And he's a genius. He's going to go to Oxford and do all these important things, and he's never coming back."

Maybe she's a little bit dramatic, but maybe she's a little bit right too. It would be one thing if Five was normal. If he was in high school with her. If he took her to all those high-school things and they grew into adulthood together. But he's not. He's Five. And he's been an adult since he was… well, born. I almost laugh at that thought.

"Well," I say, letting out a sigh of defeat, "you two still have a few weeks together. So don't give up on that kiss, OK?"

She tips her head up to see if she heard me correctly.

I shrug. She knows what that means.

"I got a present for Mommy. To make her feel better. Do you want to see it?"

"Yes," I say. "I'm desperate to make her happy tonight, Princess. So if you can help me do that, I'd even let Five take you on another date."

"Really?" she almost squeals.

"With Oliver as chaperone."

"Deal! I'm so going on that second date. Because I know exactly what Mommy needs." And then she gets up and takes my hand, pulling me to my feet. "But let's sneak out the library door so I can show you. It's in Uncle Vic's truck."

We walk out the doors, down the pathway to the front of the house, and she stops at the truck door, smiling like she's got the secret of the century.

And when she opens it up and shows me the present, I smile that way too.

Because my daughter's unauthorized date with Five Aston just might fix everything.

Rory Shrike is a genius.

14

RONIN

Sparrow is… like a bird flying in the wind. That's how I pictured her when she was born. Some free-flying spirit with her mother's beauty and her father's… well, I'm not sure she's got anything of value from me. That makes me smile as I watch her flit around on stage, playing the part of one of the party kids in act one of *The Nutcracker*.

She's danced in this production up here in Vail since she was four and down in Denver since she was seven. Well, it wasn't dancing way back then. It was sitting on stage dressed up like a piece of candy. But she stuck it out. She did the work, took all the classes, and got the pointe shoes.

So this year it pays off. Party kid in act one and a Chinese dancer in act two. That's one of the songs everyone thinks of when you say *Nutcracker*.

Sparrow was beyond thrilled.

Hell, I'm beyond thrilled. Even if I didn't realize it until this very second.

During intermission we get up and mingle, but I know Rook's mind is only on Sparrow. I walk up to her and Starling with drinks from the bar. Ford and Spencer come with us to this show every year. It's become a tradition. Like decorating the cookies afterward. Like coming up here to the mountains for Christmas every year. We only stay the two nights. Spencer and Ronnie take the kids to the grandparents down in Park Hill on Christmas Day. Rook and I see Elise, Antoine, and their three kids, who are all the right ages to play with my brood. And Ford and Ash take their kids to Mrs. Aston's where Sasha and Jax turn up with Lauren and little Matthew for the family party at night.

But Christmas Eve has always been a day in the life of the Team. An epilogue to the stories we wrote all year. A time to just be ourselves. To take stock of what we did, how big our kids got, where we're headed.

I know where I'm headed. Home.

I don't know if I work too much, but clearly I'm not paying enough attention. Clearly I'm taking for granted the one thing I have as an adult that I never had as a kid.

A traditional family.

How did it become so easy to take it all for granted?

After intermission we all pile back into the Team row in the theatre.

Rook is practically crying before the lights even go out. But it's a happy, happy cry. I reach over and squeeze her hand just as the second act begins. She looks up at me and breathes in deeply. "God, Ronin. How did she get so big, so fast?"

I shrug and give her hand another squeeze as my answer. She leans her head against my shoulder as we watch, eagerly waiting for Sparrow to come on stage again.

Starling climbs over the armrest, leaving the bouquet of roses we brought for Sparrow in her empty seat, and settles in my lap. She's tired from skiing. Ballet is not her thing. Oh, she loves to see Sparrow do it. But she doesn't dream of sugarplums. She dreams of, well... skiing, I guess.

"Tired, Star?" I ask.

"Mmm-hmm," she moans into my tux.

Sparrow's dance goes perfectly in my eyes, but I know her well enough to anticipate the critique of her performance afterward. She's a perfectionist.

Maybe that's what she gets from me? Maybe that's what drives Star to that daredevil stuff she does out on the slopes? Maybe I did have a hand in all this success even though I let work become a priority and I've missed some of it the past year.

Rook squeezes my hand this time. "She looks just like you, Ronin. Just like you." Her eyes find mine and she leans up, ever so slightly, and her lips brush my cheek. "Mr. Flynn," she says in a deep throaty voice. "I think we should skip out on cookie decorating. I have a surprise for you."

I waggle my eyebrows at her. I know what that means. I laugh out loud a little and Starling wakes up long enough to say, "Shush, Daddy."

We watch the rest of the performance and when an exhilarated, but very tired, Sparrow comes out the lobby after all the post-show festivities are done, we give her the roses and then walk hand in hand as a family back to our car.

The mansion comes to life after the show, even though it is almost midnight. There are dozens of cookies to be decorated before bed. There's hot chocolate, and hot cider to be consumed. There's the customary Christmas Eve gift to be handed out.

It's always been like this. It's like we never want this day to end. And if we could pack even more stuff into it, make it last longer, make it last forever, we would.

Rook and I stay just long enough to get everyone settled, and then I take her hand and lead her upstairs. I catch a wink from Ronnie that says, *We've got your back,* and then the noise from below recedes.

"We could've waited," Rook says breathlessly as I close our bedroom door and twist the lock.

"No," I say back. "We've got hours of things to do, and Mrs. Flynn, I'd die if I didn't have a moment alone with you right this second. I just want to say, I'm sorry I've been working so much."

"Ronin," she starts.

But I put a finger to her lips to keep her quiet. "Shh," I whisper, my hands sliding underneath her shirt and up her back.

She buckles away from me, squealing, "They're cold!"

"They won't be cold for long," I say, biting her lip and

giving her a kiss. "Now what sort of surprise did you have in mind?"

"One second," she says, holding up a finger. She turns and goes over to the refrigerator we keep for adult drinks. Her dress is red tonight. Rook always wears something red on Christmas Eve. Sometimes it's just a scarf, sometimes it's her coat, sometimes it's a ribbon in her hair. But this Christmas Eve, it's a dress. A very fucking sexy dress.

That she starts to take off. She slides the straps slowly down her arms and I untuck my white dress shirt and start unbuttoning it from the bottom up.

She grins at me, a small squeak of delight escaping her lips as she shimmies her dress over her hips and stands there in her black bra and panties.

I grin back as I take my shirt off and go for my belt buckle.

Her eyes never leave my fingers as I tug the zipper down and step out of my pants.

We stand there in our underwear for a few moments before we take that off too.

We stand there naked, looking each other up and down, appreciating each other the way we always do on Christmas Eve, and then Rook gets the bottle of champagne from the mini fridge and grabs two glasses from the side table. Her walk towards the terrace is seductive as fuck.

"What?" I laugh.

"Remember when you took me to the zoo for that charity event?"

I can't help but smile. "We'd just met and Antoine and Elise gave us their tickets so we could have a date together."

"That was the best night of my life, Mr. Flynn. Well, up to that point. But every night since then has been the best night of my life. Every night I climb into bed I think, *How did I get so lucky?*"

"It's not luck, Rook. It's love."

"I know. Humor me," she says, popping the cork on the champagne and pouring it into the glasses. "Every morning when I wake up I think, *God, I can't wait to get back in bed with him tonight.* I just can't wait. It's the very best part of every single day since we met. Even after fifteen years, I still think that, Ronin." She grabs two coats off one of the chairs next to the door and hands me mine. "Don't ask, just put it on."

We slip them on at the same time, our eyes glued to each other. I want to kiss her so bad, but she's got a hand on my chest as she holds out a glass of champagne for me to take.

I take it. Reluctantly. I just want to take her. Every part of her.

She holds her own glass of champagne in one hand, then takes my free one in her other and pulls me over to our balcony. She opens the door and the softly falling snow comes in as we go out.

She closes the door behind us and then we're in the dark. Only the lights from Vail Village leak up to our little piece of the mountain to illuminate us.

"That very first Christmas we spent together. Do you remember that present Ford gave me after church?"

"Eric Cartman." I laugh.

"Yeah," Rook says, like she's remembering it fondly. "Well, I was talking on the phone to Ford to say thank you, and I was telling him that story about what I was doing on Christmas Eve the year before. And I told him I was wishing on a star to make my life change. Just anything, you know. I just needed to leave that bad situation and start fresh."

"Yeah," I say, thinking back to that first year we were together. It was tough. We all had a past that was catching up with us.

"Well, every Christmas Eve since then I go out into the night after everyone is asleep and I wish on my star again. Only instead of begging for a change, I beg for more of the same."

God, I love her.

"I don't ask for perfection, Ronin. I don't ask for more money or a bigger house. I don't ask for pretty things or gifts. I don't ask for anything but more of the same. Because every moment with you is perfect, even when it's not."

I open my mouth to talk, but she shushes me again. "I don't want you to apologize for providing for us, Ronin. I don't want you to feel like you've missed things. I don't want you to be anything or anyone but who and what you are. Because you're perfectly imperfect and I don't need perfection. I just need more of the same." And then she raises her glass and says, "Cheers to us, Ronin. We made it. We started this life with everything against us, but we made it."

"Cheers to us," I say back, gazing into those blue eyes that electrified me so long ago. "I wouldn't change a minute, Gidget. So cheers to us."

"And I love," she says, just before she's about to take a drink, "that you let me call you Larue, even though everyone knows you wanted to be Gidget."

Yes, I think as I laugh. *I might not be perfection, but she certainly is.*

She's certainly perfect for me.

"I have a present for you, Larue." She hands me her glass of champagne and walks over to the hot tub and flips the lid over, then eases it all the way off. The steam rises up in waves and swirls as it mingles with the cold mountain air.

"Get in," she says, walking back over to me and taking both glasses from me. I take off my coat, drape it over a chair, and then get in, hissing as the hot water comes in contact with my skin. She hands me back both glasses and then walks over to the little black case and produces a portable projection machine. She inserts a flash drive and smiles at me over her shoulder.

"What are you up to?" I laugh.

"You'll see," she says, finishing up and walking back to me. She slips her coat off, piles it on top of mine, and then eases down into the water next to me, taking her glass back. She's got a small remote control in her hand that she clicks, and then the side of the house comes to life with a movie.

"What did you do?"

"I made us a movie." She laughs. "I don't make many these days, but I got an idea last Christmas. I knew then that the kids were growing up too fast, so I spent all year putting this together. And maybe we don't have all our special moments in here, but we've got enough, Ronin."

The film starts and it's the movie I made the day Sparrow was born. Ford and Spencer are there. Ashleigh and Veronica. Five is still small in Ashleigh's arms, and Kate is clinging to Ford. Spencer is holding a Cinderella version of Rory, and Veronica is leaning over Rook, cooing down at Sparrow.

"That's when it became real, you know?" Rook is looking at me with wide blue eyes. "Our wedding was the start, but Sparrow was when it became real."

I totally get it. "Yeah," I say back softly. "She made us real."

"And every day after that just got better and better, Ronin. So I put it all together into a movie for us. So no matter how fast they grow, we'll always have this to remind us of what it was like in the beginning."

15

FORD

"Ford," Spencer calls across the great room. We put all the kids except Cindy to bed an hour ago, but Spencer had exactly seventeen toys that need assembly. Somehow he got the impression that I am part of his production line.

"No," I deadpan back at him. Five was never into toys that needed to be put together. He liked musical things. Puzzles and computer games. And Kate, well, she did like that stuff, but she grew out of dollhouses by the time she was eight. After that it was all horses all the time. She got a new horse last year. Charlie. And she's not ready to upgrade. So this year she's getting gear from that equestrian catalog the girls will be modeling for. "I already put together the Tiny Town Garage, the Tiny Town Hair Salon, and the Tiny Town Pet Groomer. I'm on strike."

"We're done, dude. I was just going to ask if you guys could watch Cindy for a few hours."

"It's two AM. What kind of child needs watching—"

"Yes," Ashleigh says, already on her feet, reaching for Cindy. "We'd love to. Go see what Veronica's doing."

"Thanks, man," Spencer says to me, like I'm the one doing him a baby favor.

Rook and Ronin are already in bed, so now it's just me, Ashleigh, and the third wheel. "Well," I say, taking a sip of Scotch as I glance at Cinderella. What kind of name is that? I don't even bother. Spencer took his pack of princesses way too seriously. "I feel like I haven't seen you all day, Ash. I missed you."

She smiles at me. No, wait. She's smiling at Cindy.

I forgot. She wants another one.

"Ford," she says in her serious tone that means she's got something on her mind. "I think—"

"Wait," I say, stopping her mid-sentence. "I know what you're going to say. I've seen the signals."

"You have?"

"Yes. You're sad that the kids are growing up and you want another one. I get it, Ash. And I know why you haven't made a big deal about it all these years. I appreciate that, you know."

"Yeah, but Ford—"

I put another hand up. "Ashleigh, wait. I'm just saying that I sorta agree."

"You do?" Her eyes go wide.

"Yeah. Kate, man." I have to laugh. I told Ashleigh what she did on the slopes today. We are alike in that respect. We get a kick out of all the strange stuff our children do. Most parents would be upset about their fifteen-year-old practically kidnapping a princess and taking her all over Colorado. And we gave him a stern talking-to about that when he got home. The whole united front thing. He's in charge of shoveling the driveway tomorrow morning before we leave to go to my mother's.

But secretly we love how innovative he is. And Kate. She lights up my life. I don't know how all these years got away from me. I don't understand how she went from footied sleepers to selling ski lessons to buy a car. It doesn't make sense.

"I'm with you, Ashleigh. If you want a baby, I'm ready to make another one."

She laughs.

"What?"

"Who says that? Make another one?"

"What? That's how it happens."

"OK, never mind," she says, still shaking her head. Cindy is half asleep, but fighting it hard. Her teething seems to be under control, but now her schedule is all off. "But that's not what I was going to say."

"What? I thought you had empty-nest syndrome? I thought you were craving another baby? I thought you missed all the spit-up, the dirty diapers, and the constant neediness?"

"Well, that's all sorta true."

"Then why have you been acting weird?"

She shoots me a sly grin. "I can't believe you haven't noticed."

"Noticed what?" I ask, taking another sip of my drink.

"My candy pussy."

And my fifty-year-old Scotch goes shooting out my mouth. "What did you just say, Miss Li? I might owe you a spanking for that remark."

She laughs hard. Hard enough to wake up Cindy from her almost-slumber. Cindy quickly gets a cuddle to soothe her back to sleep.

Once that crisis is averted, I get another giggle. "I'm pregnant, Ford. I took the test last week and I didn't know how to tell you, so I've been trying to keep it a secret until tonight. And holy shit, you are so off your game. I can't believe you ate me out last night and didn't even notice."

Fuck. When was the last time Ashleigh and I had a conversation about candy pussy? Back when she was pregnant with Five, I guess. We have sex six times a week, at least. And at least two of those are of the naughty variety. But holy shit, she knows exactly what to say to spice things up. She's always known exactly what to say. It's so easy for her to make me happy. "Mrs. Aston, you are my soulmate. I love the fact that you remember how much I love your candy pussy. And…"

And… this is the part she's been waiting for. The part where I react to her news. Considering that I've been against the idea for fifteen years, I'm not surprised she was acting strange all week. "And I know it's my fault we don't have more, but now really is the perfect time."

I get up and walk over to her. She's sitting on the floor in front of the tree, cradling Cindy in her arms. So I sit down next to her and take the baby. Trying it on for size again.

Cindy squirms, but I place her up close to my chest the way I used to hold Kate. The way I used to hold Five. And she rests her heavy head on my shoulder.

"Yes," I say. "I'd like another Kate. I'm not ready to grow up yet."

"Good," Ashleigh says, her eyes bright with mischief. "Because we're having twins."

SPENCER

I walk upstairs, my mind on the Bomb and what's about to happen, when my eyes wander to the thin slice of light leaking from under the door to the attic stairs.

Five, I say in my head. I was so mad at him. I was almost ready to overstep my bounds in the library a few hours ago.

But my princess. I sigh. Whatever it is they feel for each other, it feels real to them. My thoughts wander back to when I first fell in love. God, I did some stupid things. It feels like it was yesterday when I snuck into that apartment James sent Ronnie to after her old one was... declared uninhabitable. I probably owe James a drink for that, now that I think about it fifteen years later.

But everything when you're young is so immediate. And when you're a teenager, it's so much *more* immediate.

I knock on the door to the attic and open it up before

anyone answers. The boys might've fallen asleep with the light on, but somehow, I don't think so.

When I climb the last step and peek around the wall, I'm right. Oliver is asleep. He's snoring with an R2D2 blanket all wrapped around his legs.

But Five is awake.

As soon as he realizes it's me he takes a deep breath. Like he's steadying himself. "I'm sorry, Mr. Shrike," he says. "You have every right to be angry with me."

The Mr. Shrike typically comes off condescending when Five says it. But not this time. And this kid, he's never been afraid of me. I'm sure he's much more afraid of Ronnie's brother Vic than he is me. But this time it comes off as... sincere.

"I was talking to Rory earlier."

He swallows.

"And she said she had a real nice time with you today. Except for one part."

His eyebrows shoot up. This time, it's in surprise. "She didn't care for something we did today?" I shake my head and let out a long breath. Five's face falls, like he's a complete failure. "Did she say which part?"

He sounds defeated. Like he did his best and it wasn't good enough. "She did," I say back.

"Do you mind telling me what it was? Just so..." He stops and looks out the window, like he's imagining another day in his mind. A day where he gets it all right. "So I know how to make her happy if I ever get a next time?"

"She said she didn't get a kiss goodnight."

His smile starts small, but it grows so big in the span of a few moments, he has to turn his head to hide it.

"She said she's sad, Five."

He turns back to me, his smile gone now.

"She thinks you're going to forget about her."

"I won't," he insists.

I nod, agreeing with him. But my Baby Bomb is smarter than the rest of us. Because he will. She's right, he will. It can't be helped. "Sometime," I say, thinking about Ronnie earlier in the day and the present that Rory brought home tonight, "sometimes there is only one thing that can make a person feel better. One *person*. Love does that to you. And right now, the only thing that will make her believe that you will be back is a kiss. So you have my permission."

He stares at me with his mouth open. In fact, we stare at each other for several seconds in silence.

"Did you hear me?"

He nods.

"But I have conditions, Aston. Don't—"

"I won't," he interjects.

"—hurt her," I finish. "And keep your hands—"

"I promise," he says, standing up so he can look me in the eye.

"—above the shoulders."

"I promise, Spencer. I'll do it right."

I nod at him, and then turn to go back down the attic stairs. But then I realize what I really want to say and stop one more time. "Just make her happy, Five. That's all I want. Just make her happy."

I walk back down after that, feeling like this is the end of something. Or at the very least, the beginning of the end. Princess Rory's childhood, I guess. It's the beginning of the end of her childhood.

How does it go by so fast?

That thought is still on my mind when I get to our bedroom door. The lights are on, but Ronnie's not awake. She's all curled up in a chair over by the bay windows, a red blanket wrapped around her body. The red blanket is good luck, I realize.

"Bombshell," I whisper, leaning down into her ear. "Wake up."

"Hmm?" she mumbles as I swoop her up in my arms. "What's going on?"

I don't say a word. Just carry her out the bedroom door and down the back staircase.

"Spencer?" she asks, as we get to the bottom of the steps. She's so tired it took her all that time to properly wake up. "Where are we going?"

"You'll see," I say back, walking down the long hallway that leads to the indoor pool. We are accosted with the smell of chlorine as I kick the swinging doors open with one foot and carry her over to a long patch of fake grass near the doors that lead to the outside.

I set her down and her legs straighten so she can hold herself up. But her eyes are everywhere. She's looking at everything I have laid out on the grass.

"It's a stupid inside pool and not a buckeye tree. Plus the grass is fake, so it hardly counts. But I was informed by our daughter that this is what you need to snap out of your funk. She went and picked it up from the shop when she was in Fort Collins with Five today."

Ronnie's still looking at all my supplies as I finish this statement. But then she looks up and her lip trembles. "You're going to… paint me?"

At first I think it was a mistake because of the trembling lip and the threat of tears. But then I realize they are good tears. The smile is late to the party, but another moment and it's there too.

"Rory did this?" she asks.

I nod. "She's got you pegged, Bombshell." And then I let out a laugh of relief.

"We had fun, didn't we, Spencer?"

We're caught in the same moment from the past. The day I painted her up as a fairy and we waited for nightfall so I could take her picture as we made love under the moonlight. It was in my gran's old atrium. The one I had to demolish in order to save the buckeye tree trapped under the glass.

"We're still having fun, Veronica. I think you just need to be reminded. So I'm gonna do one more masterpiece on your beautiful body. And then I'm going to fuck the shit out of you as the camera takes our picture."

She throws the blanket off and stands there on the grass in a pink and white nightie. "What will you paint on me, Spencer?"

"You'll have to wait and see. Now sit here and eat cookies."

She smiles and a chuckle bursts forth. But she takes a seat next to the plate of newly decorated cookies, and picks one up that says, *Mommy.*

"I know baking cookies makes you happy. And I'm pretty sure eating cookies makes everyone happy. So you're gonna sit here and eat cookies and be happy." She looks up at me, those bombshell eyes finally—*finally*—bright again. "Because if you're not happy, then I've failed you, Veronica Shrike. And I'm not a guy who likes to fail."

She draws in a deep breath. "Do you want me naked?"

"I always want you naked."

She pulls the nightie over her head and then slips her matching panties down her legs. "I'm ready then."

"Me too."

I've never painted this design on her and looking back, I should've. I should've done it a long time ago. I start with the airbrush filled with black paint and before long, her thighs look like latex. Her arms are kept bare, but her middle becomes a red corset, painted to perfectly accentuate her amazing cleavage and waist, complete with little satin ribbons crisscrossing their way up her stomach until it looks like the corset is so tight, her girls are spilling out.

I give her red boots that end just past her knees, and golden bracelets that I stole from Wonder Woman.

I paint a white triangle on her bosom, and she breathes

deeply as she waits to see what I will put in the center of the diamond of white.

An S, of course. In the Shrike Bikes font.

"S for Shrike?" she asks.

But I shake my head as I clean up the airbrush, put everything away, and then take out the camera and set it up on the tripod.

I silently drape the red blanket over her shoulders and fasten it at her neck with a ducky-headed diaper pin. No," I finally answer her question as I take off my shirt, unbuckle my belt, and let my pants drop to the ground. "An S for super. Supermom," I say. "Superwife," I whisper as I walk towards her and wrap my arms around her middle.

The camera starts beeping in intervals, just like it did back when we were in college.

"Superbomb," I say, right into her mouth as I kiss her. "You're my Super Bomb. You're perfect. And I love every inch of you. I don't ever want you to forget that, Mrs. Shrike."

The real smile appears then. The one I was looking for all day each time my eyes found hers. The smile that says we still like all the same things. We still like our farm, and our pack of children, and the pound puppies we've adopted over the years. We still like the buckeye tree, and motorcycles, and leather jackets.

We still like each other. We still like each other and it will always be that way.

FIVE

I text Rory from the great room, standing in front of the tree. *Come down here,* I say. *And bring your phone.*

But I don't get an answer. She might be asleep.

I hear a creak on the old wooden stairs and my eyes shoot up to the top, where Princess Rory Shrike stands in a pink nightgown that almost reaches to the floor. I'm still wearing my suit from the ballet tonight, and it feels wrong somehow. Kate was right, the suit is all wrong.

She is still a girl and I already feel like a man. It will never work out the way we want it to. It will never be the same once I go to school for real.

But then she smiles and her feet are flying down the steps. "What are you doing out here, Five?" She's beaming with happiness, and it makes me feel like every doubt I just had was false. That we do have a chance, but we have to take it now. It makes me feel like this is our one moment to get it right.

I'm going to do it right, I silently promise her.

"I talked to your dad a few minutes ago."

"Oh, my God, what did he say?" But she's not worried about what he said. She's excited that we are down here alone. That we aren't done with each other yet.

"He said," I say, my own excitement building with hers, "you were disappointed with something."

"I loved our date, Five. Every minute. I'm not disappointed."

"No?"

She shakes her head and her golden-blonde hair shakes with it.

"So you weren't unhappy that we didn't get our first kiss?"

She covers her mouth with her hand, but that smile— that smile that will keep me going for the rest of my days— peeks through her fingertips.

"Because I would very much like my first kiss to be with you, Princess. In fact, I can't possibly have a first kiss with any other girl. It would spoil my whole life."

This makes her draw in a deep breath. "I'd never kiss anyone, ever, if you left me without doing it, Five."

We stare at each other for a few moments. I want that kiss so badly. But I have something else for her first. "I got you a present. Give me your phone."

She looks down at her phone like she's just remembered she has it in her hand. But then she holds it out for me and I take it. I flick away her sleep screen and take a small hard drive out of my suit pocket. I plug her phone into it and she looks at me quizzically.

"What are you doing?"

"I made this app and I was going to release it on Valentine's Day. It's for people who want to say mushy things to someone they like, but don't know how to say them. It's called Love Notes. But I decided I'm not going to release it. I made it for us. I'm giving it to you so whenever you get lonely or wish I was here, all you have to do is push a button and it will send me a love note."

"I don't even have to write it?"

"Nope," I say. "And that may sound like it's not personal, but it is, Rory. Because I wrote all the love notes myself and I wrote every one with you and me in mind. So if you send me one, I'll know it's real. And if I send you one, you'll know it's really from me. It's just for us." I look at her as the phone beeps, and then I disconnect the two devices and hand hers back. She takes it in her palm, and our hands touch, making an electric feeling shoot up my arm.

We lock eyes and I keep my promise to Spencer and place my hands on her shoulders as I lean in.

She holds her breath as our lips touch.

It's a small kiss. It's a teenage kiss. It's a first kiss.

But it's all the things that make a kiss perfect.

"I made it for us, Rory. Because I'm going to make sure, no matter what happens, there will always be an us."

**CONTINUE THE STORY OF THE ROOK & RONIN
KIDS BY STARTING THE MISTERS!**

**Five , Oliver and baby Cinderella all have their own
books! Rook & Ronin gang show up too!**

Seven books - the complete series.
THE MISTERS BOX SET

MR. PERFECT

Ellie is the "celebrity concierge" at Stonewall Entertainment. She's good at it. On most days. Just not the day her new boss, McAllister Stonewall, shows up and catches her secretly sexting in his debut executive meeting.

MR. ROMANTIC

Ivy is the "preacher's daughter" and she's desperate for a job when a sweet opportunity comes in from the infamous Mr. Romantic. Nolan Delaney might be deliciously hot, but he's got a dark side lurking under that charm.

MR. CORPORATE

West wants a girl who needs him and Victoria can handle things just fine on her own, thank you. But now that West is back, so are all her old secrets. Like it or not, she might need him to save her.

MR. MATCH (Cinderella's Book)

Cindy does not give a crap about the best-friend's-little-sister rule. She wants Mr. Mysterious all to herself. He's dangerous, and moody, and probably shouldn't be drinking whiskey for breakfast. But lucky him—she's willing to be his partner. Everyone needs a team, right? She's not afraid of a little scandal.

MR. MATCH (Oliver's Book)

Katya is a girl with secrets. Is she a Russian spy? A liar? Or just a lost girl who fell in love with the "right" wrong man? Meeting Mr. Match four years ago changed her whole life. Who knew fate would intervene just when all hope was lost? But she should've known better. She doesn't deserve him.

MR. FIVE (Five's Book)

Rory and Five were best friends, childhood sweethearts, and the definition of soul mates. Nothing could ever come between them. Except Five thinks she's better off without him. But Rory Shrike wants her man back. And not even the genius brain of Mr. Five will stop her.

MR. & MRS.

(All the misters and Rook & Ronin gang show up!)

Is it the wedding of the century? Or a disaster in the making? All the Misters are gathered together on Five's island paradise for the most outrageous wedding in the history of weddings.

Series is Complete!

END OF BOOK SHIT

END OF BOOK SHIT

Well, shit. Going back into this world was the best. I had the most fun writing these seventeen chapters and I fell right back into their make believe lives. Its feels short to me. It went by so fast, but that was the idea. Just a little epilogue to see how the whole Team fared at the game of life. We should be so lucky, right?

So I hope you enjoyed this little Christmas story. It's really hard for me to decide on a favorite part because it seems like every single chapter had some little gem that just made me smile. Kate was the biggest surprise. She was so small in Ford's book and in Guns. She really had no personality, just a heavy genetic inheritance. So I love, love, loved her chapter at the ski slopes. It really shows whose daughter she really is. Ford's. For sure. His mini-me, even though at first glance, everyone thinks that title goes to

Five. He'd like another Kate. And good thing too. Twins, right? Ford can't do anything without overachieving. Plus, Ashleigh deserves another round of babies. She met Ford and a year later was settled with 2.5 kids, a house, and a pack of face-eating dogs. Did she slip up on her pill? I'd like to think so.

And Spencer, so perfect as always. It took me a while to come up with the right gift to make Ronnie feel better. I was saying the same thing in my head as Rory was. There is nothing in any of those Village shops that will make Ronnie feel special. I almost did give them the limo, but what kind of people keep a limo driver on call on Christmas Eve? Not Ford and Ashleigh. ;) So the body painting was really the only way to set her right. I always pictured Spencer as a family man and it's so much karma that he got four little princesses before he got *his* mini me, Oliver. But his girls will know how to change the oil on a bike and they will pass down all those Small Frye boots until the soles fall off. I think I love Spencer the most. And that's funny, I barely liked him in Tragic. I never thought he could carry a book. But people started asking about him almost immediately and with each part he played, I loved him a little more. "Tell me what we like, Bombshell," is still one of my most favorite scenes ever.

Rory was exactly how I pictured her – Princess, right? But don't let her fool you, there's a lot more going on in that head than cheerleading and horseback riding. There's more to her than blonde hair and big tits. She's the original

Baby Bomb and she takes after her mother in more ways than one. ;)

I love that Ronin had a little life check. Does he work too much? I doubt it, but who cares. I'm sure Sparrow and Starling are grateful I gave him a mini mid-life crisis so they get to see him more. And the modeling—well, Sparrow is too smart to bank on her beauty. I bet she does become a veterinarian. I love that Rook found her voice and stood up for what she and the girls needed from Ronin. Rook has come a long, long way from Tragic and she probably has the near-perfect version of the HEA.

I love that Ford did all he wanted to do with the movie production stuff. I love that he quit doing it on his own, even before he realized he was just bored. And I love that he and Ashleigh started skiing after things settled down back when the kids were little. I picture Ford taking those kids to the Olympics one day. I think Olympic ski coach suites him. Maybe he will make that documentary? I'd watch it.

And how fitting that this books ends the team right back where Rook started it. Lots of things happened on Christmas Eve in these books. Rook decided to wish on a star back when she was with Jon. Ford met Sasha and had that whole day in a life Slack book. Ashleigh, if you were paying attention, got off her plane from Japan with baby Kate on Christmas Eve, the same one where Ford was having a Rook crisis. And James and Harper took Sasha to live with Ford on Christmas Eve after all that Dirty, Dark, and Deadly stuff was over.

And Five. Is he the New Ford? You'll have to wait and see. There will be a full-length, standalone book about Five and Rory once they grow up (next spring, 2016). I can't wait.

I hope you all have a Merry Christmas. Thanks for reading, thanks for reviewing, and thanks for making 2015 spectacular. See you in the next book!

Julie

CONTINUE THE STORY OF THE ROOK & RONIN KIDS BY STARTING THE MISTERS!

Five , Oliver and baby Cinderella all have their own books! Rook & Ronin gang show up too!

Seven books - the complete series.

ABOUT THE AUTHOR

JA Huss is a scientist, New York Times and USA Today bestselling author. Her self-published romantasy Sparktopia was named an Audible Editors' Best of the Year selection in 2024, and several of her audiobooks have been nominated for the Audie and SOVA Awards. A 2019 RITA finalist, Huss has also had five books optioned for film and television.

Get FREE AUDIOBOOKS and
enter to win giveaways on my WEBSITE.
AMA in my READER GROUP - SHRIKE BIKES - on
Facebook - Get all my new releases early on PATREON